"I won't be tied to you for the rest of my life."

Her voice trembled with tears. "You can't keep me here against my will."

"Perhaps it won't be against your will." Jordan's gray eyes narrowed on the parted softness of her mouth, his meaning clear.

Lise flinched. Of course he knew that she loved him. She had given herself away so many times.

Jordan bent his dark head, kissing her deeply, sweetly. "You're my wife, Lise," he told her. "And I want you!"

"No," she protested bitterly. "I'm not your wife. Our marriage is a joke. No—a business deal. The joke is on me. Well, you may have bought Holbrook International, but you haven't bought me!"

PATRICIA LAKE started reading romances when she worked as a library assistant in Birmingham, England. She didn't start writing, however, until she moved to the Yorkshire countryside. Her first book was completed in record time and when it was accepted for publication, she knew she'd found her niche in life.

Books by Patricia Lake

HARLEQUIN PRESENTS
465—UNTAMED WITCH
501—PERFECT PASSION
521—WIPE AWAY THE TEARS
538—HEARTLESS LOVE
570—A STEP BACKWARDS
578—THE SILVER CASKET
593—MOMENT OF MADNESS
634—FATED AFFAIR
707—ILLUSION OF LOVE
730—FIDELITY
907—DARK BETRAYAL

Don't miss any of our special offers. Write to us at the following address for information on our newest releases.

Harlequin Reader Service
901 Fuhrmann Blvd., P.O. Box 1397, Buffalo, NY 14240
Canadian address: P.O. Box 603,
Fort Erie, Ont. L2A 5X3

PATRICIA LAKE

fascination

Harlequin Books

TORONTO • NEW YORK • LONDON
AMSTERDAM • PARIS • SYDNEY • HAMBURG
STOCKHOLM • ATHENS • TOKYO • MILAN

Harlequin Presents first edition June 1987
ISBN 0-373-10986-5

Original hardcover edition published in 1986
by Mills & Boon Limited

CHAPTER ONE

LISE studied her face without concentration as she quickly stripped off the heavy theatrical make-up.

She felt tired, drained of emotion after the performance—the last performance. The play had closed tonight—the final curtain had gone down some thirty minutes ago—and mingled with her exhaustion and the elation that performing brought, there was a kind of sadness. She had become used to Melissa, the hard, bitchy and brilliant character she had been playing every night for the past six months. It had been a difficult part, but the few reviews that had mentioned her had been good.

'What are you wearing for the party?' Jerri grabbed the jar of cold cream from over her shoulder and began scrubbing at her face. Fashion was one of Jerri's passions; she had more clothes than anyone else Lise had ever known.

'I'm not going,' said Lise firmly, tightening the belt of her wrap around her narrow waist.

Jerri's hand stopped mid-way between the jar of cream and her face. '*What*? Of course you are—everybody's going!' Her voice was shocked, incredulous, her brown eyes wide.

The two girls had shared the cramped, shabby dressing-room since the play opened, and had become firm friends. Jerri was small and pretty with raven hair. Her tongue could be sharp or witty or friendly, and she was married to the play's producer, Nick Carvallo. Her next part was already lined up—she had

walked her audition the week before—so her mood
tonight was high and cheerful. Lise, on the other hand,
was facing a period of unemployment—or resting, as
it was delicately referred to. This had been her first
part in a major play since leaving drama school. She
had failed two auditions and she hadn't heard from
her agent in weeks. Consequently, she didn't feel in
the mood for a party.

'Not me.' She smiled at Jerri's horror. 'I'm for a hot
bath and an early night with a good book.'

'Oh, come on! Come with me—it'll be fun. You
can't miss the last night party! Nick is expecting you
to be there. And besides, it's bad luck.' Jerri wheedled
away persuasively, as she pulled her black hair into a
high ponytail.

'You'll be with Nick,' replied Lise smiling. 'And I
hate parties.'

That was true. She did hate them. By nature she was
shy and sensitive, and it had been at a party that . . .
She pushed ths thought away, her hand trembling.

'So I've noticed.' Jerri sighed, eyeing her critically.
'You're far too serious, darling, but I'm not going to let
you wriggle out of this one.'

'But I've got nothing to wear.' It was a last weak
protest. Having decided that afternoon not to go, she
hadn't brought a suitable dress, and her old jeans and
T-shirt wouldn't do.

But Jerri was strong-minded. She had made her
mind up that Lise was going to the party, and she
always got her own way. She and Nick lived in a kind
of fiery harmony. Jerri was twenty-five, four years
older than Lise, and she'd been married for eighteen
months. Lise had heard her and Nick rowing, in this
very dressing-room: it had been quick and violent and
passionately made up. Jerri was a whirlwind of energy

and enthusiasm, and Lise half envied her ability to rush headlong through life, grabbing everything she wanted.

'No problem, I've got loads of stuff here.' Opening the wardrobe, Jerri flicked through a stack of dresses, all carefully covered with polythene. 'I didn't know what sort of a mood I'd be in after the performance, so I played safe,' she admitted cheerfully. 'Lucky, we're about the same size.'

Inwardly sighing, Lise said nothing, but brushed out her shoulder-length hair. It lay loose and thick around her neck, the silvery softness, expertly cut in a thick wedge, falling over her pale cheeks when she bent her head.

'Here you are. This will suit you perfectly.' Jerri triumphantly pulled out a thin black dress—silk that glittered with hundreds of tiny beads. The neckline and back plunged in black folds. It was sexy, revealing, very fashionable, and totally unlike anything Lise would have bought for herself.

'I can't wear that!' she exclaimed, aghast.

'You'll look fantastic,' Jerri assured her. 'And I'll do your face as well.' She eyed the younger girl critically. 'You don't make the best of yourself, darling. You're really quite stunning.'

Damned with faint praise, Lise thought, with a wry smile.

'Jerri, look, I'm not really keen——' she began again, but it was no use. Jerri was fired by the idea, and Lise found herself watching in the mirror as the older girl's skilful fingers made up her face.

She had a delicate face, the bone structure fragile beneath her pale skin. Her green eyes were widely spaced, fringed with thick lashes; her nose was straight, her mouth generous. She had been told by many men that she was beautiful, but she didn't believe it. She didn't believe a word men said. Over-familiarity with her features made her bored with herself, but surprisingly, she found herself enjoying the new look Jerri was giving her. Sparkling shadow and thick mascara accentuated her eyes, and the clever use of blusher gave her face a lean, hollow, sexy look. The final touch was lip gloss in a smouldering red.

Jerri clipped back the silvery hair with a butterfly comb and stepped back.

'There. What do you think?'

'I hardly recognise myself,' Lise laughed, turning her head to and fro to look at herself.

Jerri laughed too. 'Now try the dress.'

Lise grimaced and slid the black silk over her head. It fitted perfectly, she realised as she smoothed the soft material down over her hips. Folds of material fell low at the front and the back, leaving most of her shoulders bare, and the skirt glittered to just above her knees.

'It's outrageous,' she said, unable to stop herself smiling.

Jerri whistled under her breath. 'You look fantastic—a thousand times better than I've ever looked in that dress!'

Lise stared at her own reflection. She looked good: cool and sexy—hardly recognisable. It felt good, too.

There was a knock on the dressing-room door, and Caroline and Ashley, two other members of the cast, wandered in.

'We've ordered a taxi, want to share?' Ash broke off, his eyes fixed on Lise, widening expressively. 'Wow!' he exclaimed in a low voice. 'Lise?'

She smiled. 'The very same,' she replied, pirouetting.

Ash was one of the leading members of the company, a young, powerful actor on his way to the top. He was tall, thin and dark-haired, and beneath a serious exterior he hid a wicked sense of humour. He had been pursuing Lise since their first meeting, and she had been consistently turning him down.

She liked him. He was intelligent and witty and she enjoyed his company, but she knew that Caroline considered Ash her own personal property. Ash denied it, maintaining that he and Caroline were just friends. It was probably true, but Lise had seen the look in Caroline's eyes. It said everything.

'Don't be so rude, darling,' Caroline said now, taking his arm, the gesture openly possessive.

'What?' Ash frowned, dragging his eyes away from Lise for a second to glare at her.

'Oh, I agree, it's quite a transformation,' Caroline replied smoothly, then, eyeing Lise with a spark of malice. 'You're usually such a mouse.'

Jerri laughed. 'And you're always such a bitch, Caroline,' she retorted, sticking up for Lise as always.

Caroline smiled sweetly. 'We're ready to go. The taxi will be waiting.'

'So are we,' Jerri returned the smile, taking Lise's arm as though she suspected the younger girl would try to run away. 'I don't suppose either of you has seen Nick?'

'I think I saw him leaving with Helen about fifteen minutes ago,' Caroline revealed eagerly.

'What sharp eyes you have, darling,' Jerri marvelled acidly as they left the dressing-room. 'I'll catch him at the club, I suppose.'

Shaftesbury Avenue was alive with people as they

stepped out into the warm night air. Well-dressed crowds poured from the theatres, chattering. Taxis and cars pulled away from the kerbs in streams.

The club where the cast was meeting was only ten minutes' drive across town. It was chic, expensive and rather exclusive. Lise sat down, greeting friends, and allowed Ash to get her a glass of champagne.

'Nick's certainly pushed the boat out this time,' he whispered in her ear, making her laugh.

'I thought you weren't coming,' someone said.

'Jerri persuaded me,' Lise replied.

'And you're enjoying yourself, right?' Jerri had found Nick, and they sat down beside her.

'Yes. You were right,' she admitted as she took another glass of champagne and sipped it. 'This place is very up-market.'

Nick smiled broadly. 'Only the best, my dear.'

'You won't be saying that when you get the bill,' Jerri muttered, half seriously.

The food arrived, brought by silent waiters. Melon, roast chicken and salad. Lise, still keyed up from the performance, wasn't very hungry. She looked round the room. A band played in one corner and people were dancing. Tables edged the dance floor, and laughter filled the smoky air.

Noticing the direction of her gaze, Ash touched her shoulder. 'Care to dance?'

'What about Caroline?' She looked around but could see no sign of the other girl.

'I'm asking you,' he said, pulling her to her feet.

'Okay, okay.' She couldn't help laughing as they moved towards the dance floor.

'Brute force seems to be the only way to persuade you,' Ash said, with wry humour.

Lise shook her head, her eyes suddenly very serious,

shadowed with emotion. 'I wouldn't advise it,' she said flatly.

Ash held up his hands in mock surrender. 'Joke,' he explained, smiling, though his curiosity showed.

Lise made a conscious effort to pull herself together. 'I know, I'm sorry,' she said brightly, as they began to move to the music.

'Forget it.' He eyed her narrowly, moving closer. 'Jerri's right. You're a very serious lady.'

'Am I?' That made her laugh. Perhaps she was, but she had already drunk more champagne than she should have, and the dancing and the excitement of the performance were making her feel lightheaded. She didn't feel serious at all.

The music was fast, with a deep, throbbing rhythm, and she felt herself letting go, dancing without inhibition, her body moving with sensual grace. Laughing at something Ash mouthed at her over the noise, she turned her head, some sixth sense prickling at the back of her neck. Her wide glance met a pair of serious dark grey eyes belonging to a man seated only a few yards away. He was staring at her with cool intensity, and she couldn't look away.

The laughter died in her throat, self-conscious colour pouring into her face. Her body stiffened in reflex.

He was sitting at a table near the dance floor, with a woman in a shiny gold dress, and two other people. As their eyes held, Lise felt her heartbeat speeding up, her stomach turning over.

Those grey eyes were cool and self-assured, almost expressionless, but Lise became aware of a tension, a sudden awareness snaking between them, and for a moment she felt lost, terribly disturbed by the sheer physical impact of his gaze. He was sitting in shadow, yet she got the impression of a dark, powerful face.

Ash's voice finally penetrated her chaotic thoughts, and she jumped when he touched her arm.

'What's the matter? Are you all right?'

The man was still staring at her, and she dragged her eyes away from his at last, looking into Ash's concerned face.

'I—I want to sit down. I feel a little dizzy.' She tried to laugh, but she was still shivering inside.

'Too much champagne on an empty stomach,' Ash pronounced, his hand at her elbow, as he led her back to their table. He hadn't noticed, Lise realised with relief as she accepted a cigarette. It surprised her, because it seemed to her that she had been staring into that stranger's eyes for hours. She knew that if she turned her head now, she would be able to see him. She could almost feel the probe of those dark grey eyes. He was still staring at her, she knew, but she didn't dare to turn round.

Lise felt cold, a sweet confusing excitement trembling in her stomach. She drew on her cigarette deeply, though she rarely smoked.

She had never reacted like that before. She had never looked at a man and felt her heartbeat racing away. She stubbed out the cigarette with clumsy fingers. It must be the champagne, she told herself.

Around her, the rest of the cast were enjoying the party, laughing, chatting, dancing, but Lise felt removed from it all, miles away. Her mind kept going over and over those few strange compelling moments when she had looked into a stranger's eyes and had seen herself as he was seeing her.

She was so preoccupied with her own thoughts that she was unaware of the flutter of excitement that ran through the people around her at the approach of a tall, dark-haired man.

She heard Ash whispering, 'Isn't that Jordon Hayes?' And she looked up as Nick said deferentially, 'Mr Hayes, this is an honour. Won't you have a drink with us?'

It was *him*, tall and dark, his expensively tailored dinner-jacket moulded to the powerful lines of his shoulders.

Lise looked away again, trembling. He was obviously an important man; she had never heard Nick talking in such a respectful way before. But who was he? Was he in the theatre? The name was unfamiliar to her.

Then, suddenly, he was in front of her.

'Miss Holbrook.' His voice was deep and faintly husky, his accent American.

She lifted her head in startled surprise, hot colour tinging her cheeks as her eyes met his. How did he know her name?

'I saw the play tonight,' he said, smiling slightly at her confusion, reading her question and answering it. 'You were very good.'

'I . . . I . . . Thank you,' Lise stammered, all her usual composure deserting her. She looked up at him. He was, without any doubt, the most attractive man she had ever seen. His hair was almost black, thick and vital, brushed back from his hard-boned face, touching the collar of his jacket at the back. His nose was straight, his mouth beautifully moulded, strong and sensual. But it was those clear dark grey eyes that held her, their expression serious and wise, faintly world-weary beneath thick dark brows.

As she looked at him, she felt her heart pounding. She touched the tip of her tongue to her dry lips. 'Thank you,' she said again, hearing how ridiculously breathless and stilted her voice sounded. 'I ... I'm glad you enjoyed the play.'

He smiled, about to say something when Nick hovered near again, his expression elated. 'Are you sure I can't persuade you to have a glass of champagne with us, sir?'

The man's eyes held Lise's, as he replied with cool politeness. 'I'm sorry, I have to get back to my guests.'

'Of course, of course.' Nick smiled brilliantly. 'Another time, perhaps.'

The man turned his dark head at last to look at Nick.

'Perhaps.' He smiled, his eyes meeting Lise's briefly as he inclined his head. Then he was gone, leaving her feeling strangely bereft as she watched him walking away.

He was taller than any man in the room, yet he moved with the self-assured grace of a panther. People parted to let him through, Lise noticed as she strained her eyes to get a better look at the woman who was waiting for him at his table.

She was unbearably curious, though she couldn't have said why. As she had expected, the woman was beautiful. An elegant chignon pulled her black hair from her stark, vivacious face. The gold dress clung to a voluptuous body. Lise watched her touching the man's arm as he sat down, smiling up into his dark face.

She looked away, a tiny dart of emotion piercing her heart, so wrapped up in her own thoughts that she was barely aware that Nick was talking and had to ask him to repeat himself.

'I said, you've certainly made an impression there.' He smiled broadly. 'And by the look of it, it wasn't all one-sided.'

Lise felt herself flushing. 'I don't know what you mean.'

Jerri sat down beside her. 'What I wouldn't give for half your luck,' she said dreamily.

'Not you as well!' Lise frowned. 'Who is he, anyway.'

It was as though she had pulled a gun out of her handbag and was pointing it at the rest of the party. Stunned silence reigned for a few seconds.

'You're not serious?' gasped Nick, shaking his head. 'What on earth do they teach you in drama school these days?'

Lise ignored him, turning to Jerri. 'Tell me,' she begged, smiling at Nick's outraged expression.

'Jordon Hayes comes over here and tells you that you were good tonight, and you don't know who he *is*?' demanded Jerri in astonishment.

Lise heard Ash laughing and realised that everyone at the table was listening. She racked her brains, but the name was still unfamiliar to her.

'*Who is he*?' she asked again, feeling foolish.

'Where have you been all your life?' said Jerri with amusement. 'Don't you ever read the newspapers? Jordon Hayes is one of the richest men in America. He's some sort of merchant banker, but also a great patron of the theatre. God, Lise, you can be so dim sometimes!'

Lise shrugged. 'Well, I've never heard of him,' she said, under her breath. She wasn't impressed. She had met rich men before; they left her cold. He was probably some sort of playboy, she thought distastefully, but the memory of those shadowed eyes holding hers made her stomach turn over violently.

'Play your cards right and you could have it made there,' Jerri said, that faraway look still in her eyes.

'I'm not interested,' replied Lise firmly.

Jerri's brown eyes widened in disbelief. 'Then you really are mad! Honestly, Lise, he's the most attractive man in the room. I swear if he even looked at me, I'd fall into his arms!'

Nick grabbed her left hand. 'Remember this?' He pointed to the wedding ring on her finger.

Jerri giggled. 'Now that you've reminded me, I do.'

Nick pulled a face at her, and still holding her hand, drew her to her feet. 'Come and dance, hussy.'

Lise watched them go, half envious of their close relationship, and suddenly lonely.

She turned her head, intending to talk to Ash, but found him already chatting to Caroline, who was holding his attention by stroking his cheek as she whispered to him. Perhaps tonight was the night when Caroline would finally get what she wanted. Lise hoped so. Everyone in the company had suffered from Caroline's sharp tongue as she pursued Ash without success.

With a small sigh, Lise picked up her bag and made her way to the ladies' room. The woman in the gold dress, Jordon Hayes' companion, was checking her make-up in the gilt-edged mirrors as Lise walked in. She smiled and Lise smiled back, glancing at the woman surreptitiously as she pulled a comb out of her handbag.

She was probably in her early thirties, Lise decided, very self-assured and sophisticated. Her gold dress was fantastic, obviously *haute couture*; it emphasised every curve of her body. She's everything I'm not, Lise thought, then admonished herself for thinking that way. What was the matter with her? Jordon Hayes meant nothing to her; he never would. He was a stranger, who had complimented her on her performance. Nothing more. Men had complimented her before. She had accepted the compliments coolly and then not given them a second thought.

So why was Jordon Hayes lingering in her mind like a strange hot fever? Why couldn't she stop thinking about him when she knew that after tonight she would never see him again?

The woman in the gold dress was leaving. Lise smiled, watching her go. She washed her hands and looked at her reflection in the mirror.

This was how he had seen her, she thought with wonder. He wouldn't recognise her if he saw her in the street, wearing her own clothes instead of borrowed finery. The thought disturbed her and she pushed it into the back of her mind. With a shrug of her shoulders, she picked up her handbag and left the ladies' room.

The narrow corridor that led to the stairs was thickly carpeted, and her high-heeled shoes sank into it.

There was a man leaning against the wall. He was obviously drunk and she approached to pass him with a sudden feeling of trepidation. He turned to look at her as she neared, his bloodshot eyes sliding over her with bleary insolence.

Lise kept her head down, nearly jumping out of her skin as he grabbed her arm, his fingers hot against her bare flesh.

'Hello, darling,' he leered, pulling her closer, and she could smell the raw spirit on his breath.

'Take your hand off my arm,' she said, as coolly as she could, but she was starting to shake with the memories she had fought long and hard to forget.

'I like you,' the drunk slurred, ignoring her. 'I've

been watching you all evening. You're a pretty little thing——'

'Let me go!' There was real panic in her voice now. He was hurting her arm and she felt frightened.

The corridor was deserted, well away from the main body of the club, and downstairs the music was very loud. Would anybody hear if she shouted for help?

The man swayed closer until their faces were only inches apart. Lise struggled impotently, but he was much stronger than her and he had moved, so that she was pinned against the wall.

'How about a kiss, sweetheart?' The words were almost incoherent. His hand moved on her bare shoulder in a rough exploration that froze the blood in her veins.

She could see the sweat filming his face, the hot lust in his eyes, and she felt sick, her stomach heaving. She knew that she should try to stay calm, to deal with the situation sensibly. If she didn't panic, everything would be fine. But her throat was dry, her breath trapped in her lungs, and her mind was re-living another time, three years ago, when a man had tried to force himself on her . . .

The drunk grabbed her jaw, violently twisting her head round, and Lise closed her eyes, weak with fear, suddenly finding her voice to shout, as he tried to find her mouth.

A second later he was pulled away from her with great force, and incredibly, miraculously, she was free. She leant back against the wall, somehow not surprised to see Jordon Hayes in front of her, his eyes as cold as ice.

The drunk staggered, surprised, aiming a blow that missed by a mile. Jordon Hayes smiled coldly, as he spun the man round to face him, and drove his fist against the drunk's jaw.

The man fell awkwardly to the carpeted floor, out cold, and Jordon Hayes turned to Lise, his grey eyes narrowing on Lise as he took in her shivering body, her wide tear-filled eyes and the marks along her jaw that would soon become bruises.

Lise looked up into his calm, strong face. 'Will . . . will he be all right?' she whispered ridiculously, hardly aware of what she was saying.

'Do you care?' His voice was low, strangely gentle.

'No——' The tears were suddenly pouring down her pale cheeks, relief and shocked reaction setting in.

With a muffled oath, Jordon Hayes reached for her, drawing her gently into his arms, one hand shaping her silken hair. He held her tightly as she cried. Lise clung to his wide shoulders, her head against his chest, letting the fear slowly wash away with her tears. His hard body comforted her. She felt his calm strength flowing into her veins, bringing her back to life.

Beneath her cheek, she became aware of the deep steady rhythm of his heart. The fine material of his jacket felt rough against her bruised skin, and when she breathed in deeply, she could smell the faint tang of expensive cologne, mingling with tobacco and the clean male scent of his skin.

How strange that she felt glad to be in his arms. He was as much a stranger as the drunk, yet . . . Suddenly aware of her own disturbing train of thought, Lise pulled away from him.

He let her go, watching her, as she wiped her eyes. 'Are you okay?' he asked quietly.

Embarrassed, Lise kept her head down. 'Yes, and thank you for . . . thank you for rescuing me.'

Jordon Hayes smiled. 'My pleasure. Did he hurt you?'

She shook her head, keeping her eyes firmly on her toes. He reached out, tilting up her chin with long, gentle fingers, carefully inspecting her bruised jaw. Why hadn't she fought him off? he wondered angrily; when he had arrived, she had been passive in the drunk's arms.

'You're going to have some bruises there,' he observed expressionlessly.

Lise felt his anger. 'It doesn't matter,' she said hurriedly, avoiding his eyes. 'I'm going home now, so I can put something on it when I get back.'

'I'll give you a lift,' he asserted softly.

'No, no, really, Mr Hayes, that's not necessary.'

'You know my name.' The warm charm in his smile knocked her sideways and she felt herself flushing.

'Doesn't everybody?'

He laughed. 'When we spoke before, you had no idea who I was.'

Lise smiled at him. 'I was soon enlightened!'

The drunk was coming round, groaning and holding his head. Lise looked down at him, fear lingering in her eyes. Unconsciously she moved closer to Jordon Hayes.

'I'll take you home,' he said softly. 'We can tell the manager about this guy on the way out. Do you want to press charges?'

'No,' she replied immediately.

'Sure?' He was frowning.

'Positive. It was nothing.'

He nodded, taking her arm as they walked towards the stairs.

The woman in the gold dress caught them halfway down.

'Jordon, darling, I've been looking for you everywhere!' Her accent was American too, and she eyed

Lise with undisguised curiosity and surprise for a moment, then returned her attention to Jordon Hayes.

'Rescuing damsels in distress?' she asked with amusement.

Jordon smiled. 'Not worthy of you, Diana,' he reproved mockingly, then turning to Lise, said, 'Let me introduce you. This is Diana de la Mesengère. Diana—Lise Holbrook. Diana is——'

'Hello,' Lise smiled nervously, not realising she was cutting him off mid-sentence. She felt embarrassingly aware of her injured jaw, and wondered what on earth Diana de la Mesengère could be thinking of her.

Diana returned the smile, her blue cat's eyes still full of amused curiosity. 'Of course—the play. I wouldn't have recognised you, my dear.' She reached up and lingeringly kissed Jordon's cheek. 'I'm leaving now, darling. I'm giving Lynette and Patrick a lift. Call me.'

Then she was gone, on a whisper of gold material and a cloud of expensive French perfume.

Lise watched her go, wondering at their relationship. Were they lovers? Looking at the man by her side, it seemed more than likely, but from the expensive rings on her wedding finger, it was equally obvious that Diana de la Mesengère was married.

It was none of her business, of course, Lise decided firmly, but she found herself unable to drag her eyes away from Jordon Hayes as he spoke briefly to the manager. She watched the manager too, a small, round, balding man. He was almost on his hands and knees, apologising profusely, obviously afraid of losing Jordon Hayes' custom. She smiled to herself as she listened to the exchange. Only the very rich and the very powerful were treated with that much respect, and it made her even more curious about Jordon Hayes, and what sort of a man he was. She watched him as he came back to her side, a tall, powerfully built man with dark hair that glinted in the overhead light.

His eyes were very serious as he looked at her, and she felt her stomach lurching violently. She lowered her eyes hurriedly, and allowed him to lead her out into the cool night air.

As the darkness touched her skin she shivered and he looked down at her. She had no coat, having borrowed all her clothes from Jerri, and the shock of the evening's events left her cold now. Before she realised what he was doing, Jordon Hayes had removed his jacket and slipped it over her shoulders. It felt heavy, still warm from his body. Lise smiled up at him shyly. 'Thank you.' He smiled back at her and as their eyes held, that tense, sensual awareness shot between them again. It was so powerful that she felt dizzy.

'I really would prefer to get a taxi, Mr Hayes,' she said in a small, nervous voice.

'Now that you know my name, use it,' he said softly, brushing back a stray tendril of hair from her forehead. The casual touch made her tremble, yet she was held still by his magnetism, by the sheer force of his charm.

'I . . . I . . .' She was flustered, confused.

'Say it.' He smiled down at her, his hand still resting lightly against her hair. 'I want to hear you say my name.'

'Jordon, please, I . . .'

His mouth twisted with amusement and satisfaction. 'Much better. And before you mention a taxi again, you'd better accept the fact that I'm taking you home.'

Before she could reply, he propelled her gently but

firmly towards a low black car.

Lise slid into the passenger seat in defeated silence. The interior was luxurious, smelling of leather and polished wood. Jordon slid in beside her seconds later. She gave him her address in Kensington, then sat in silence as the engine roared into life.

As the car shot through the almost deserted streets of the city she glanced at his hands on the steering wheel. They were strong, tanned and long-fingered, yet, despite the power in them, she could imagine them being incredibly gentle. She could imagine them against her body, and her skin prickled with worry at such a crazy thought.

She let her eyes drift upwards to his profile. It was hard and uncompromising with a well-defined jaw, shadowed hollows beneath his cheekbones, and long dark lashes veiling his eyes. He was silent, seemingly preoccupied with his own thoughts, and she could read no expression in his strong face. She looked away, disturbed by her own curiosity, filled with emotions she did not understand.

Ten minutes later, the car drew to a smooth halt outside the tall, white-painted house where she lived. The journey had taken no time at all.

Jordon Hayes turned to her in the darkness.

'Lise——' he said quietly, but she cut him off, suddenly nervous, frightened of him and of herself.

'Thanks for the lift, Mr—er—Jordon, and for everything—I—I——'

He leaned forward in silence and took her mouth in a brief, hard, devastating kiss that was over before she realised his intention. With her heart pounding, she shot out of the car as though the devil himself was at her heels. And it was only when the front door was shut behind her that she stopped running, and stood leaning back against the solid wood, touching her lips with wondering fingers. Then, suddenly and inexplicably, she burst into tears.

CHAPTER TWO

LISE had a recurring nightmare that night. It was all in slow motion, never-ending.

She jerked suddenly into consciousness with a cry, sitting up in her narrow bed, staring into the darkness with wild, frightened eyes. As she slowly realised that it was only the dream again, she reached out to turn on the bedside lamp, sinking back on the pillows with a sigh of relief.

Wiping the thin film of perspiration from her forehead, she let her eyes wander over the familiar comforting shapes of the room, and her pulse began to slow to its normal pace. She hadn't had that nightmare for three months. The incident at the nightclub had sparked it off, she supposed. It was exactly the same dream she had had periodically for the past three years; it never changed because it echoed her own experience and relentlessly took her back again and again to the life she'd left behind.

At eighteen, Lise had just finished school, and was back in San Francisco with her grandfather. She had been living there for eight years; when she was ten, her mother had died unexpectedly on the operating table while undergoing routine minor surgery. The shock had been made more unendurable by the fact that Lise had never known her father. He had walked out on her mother before Lise was born and had himself been killed in a road accident when Lise was two.

She learned later that her parents' affair had been

brief and passionate, based on a fierce desire that hadn't lasted long enough to culminate in marriage. Lise's mother had fallen deeply in love and had followed Lise's father from America, where they had met. Her father had been English, a penniless artist, and the affair had been totally disapproved of by her family. They had disowned her, and she'd had too much pride to go back when the love affair was over.

Lise always remembered her mother smiling, her eyes full of sad dreams and memories. Her sudden death had left Lise shy and withdrawn. Almost immediately she had been sent to live with her grandfather in America. Mason Holbrook was a very wealthy businessman, and Lise always suspected that he had taken her in more out of a sense of duty than for any affection he might have held for her.

Her new life in San Francisco had been alien at first. Her grandfather was kind enough in a brusque, always busy way, but during those first few years she had not seen enough of him for any real bond to grow between them. It was as though he had no idea how to deal with the young girl living under his roof. Almost immediately she had been sent away, with her cousin Meredith, to an expensive girls' school in the mid-west of America.

'You're going to need a good education, girl,' Mason had told her, sounding impossibly stern and unreachable, 'if you want to get anywhere in this world.'

She attended the school for the next seven years, only returning to California during the holidays, and then she usually brought friends with her. Mason was generous about that; his home was open to any friends she cared to invite. Lise realised later that he was probably afraid she was lonely, for he spent a lot of time abroad, holding together his huge business empire, and despite the staff, and Nancy, Mason's indispensable housekeeper, secretary and nursemaid, the huge, luxurious apartment always seemed empty when she was there alone.

The other members of the Holbrook family didn't make it any easier for her. Meredith, her cousin, was a couple of years older than Lise, important at that age because Meredith always seemed so grown up and sophisticated, and they had never been close. In fact, Meredith had been openly hostile, and jealous of Lise living with Mason, while she herself lived across town in Presidio Heights with her mother and stepfather. Even at the tender age of fourteen, Meredith had aspired to wealth. Even then she had seen Lise as her usurper to Mason's affections and vast fortune. And with Lise's arrival in San Francisco, her position had undoubtedly been weakened.

Meredith was the daughter of Mason's only son Jack, who, in his mid-thirties, had quite suddenly quit the family business and turned to religion, and who now lived in a monastery somewhere in the Himalayas. Nobody had heard from him in years, and Mason was understandably bitter.

'God knows,' he had once said to Lise, in a moment of unusual openness, 'you do your best for your kids, and what happens? They damn well turn on you! Jack, your mother—there's a streak of insanity in this family, and it certainly didn't come from me!'

Lise had listened, wide-eyed, to the outburst. She hadn't been sure what he was talking about, but she had had the distinct impression that he was angry with her.

Meredith's mother had divorced Jack, in a fit of hysterical anger, as soon as he left her and had married again almost immediately. Mason had neither time

...mpathy for her. Perhaps she realised later that ...divorce was a mistake—it meant that Mason felt ...responsibility for her—but Angela was hard-headed. She didn't give up. She was convinced that Meredith deserved Jack's share of the Holbrook family fortune, a point of view that Meredith herself wholeheartedly agreed with. And because of this constant family squabbling, Meredith had all but left Lise to fend for herself at the expensive school.

Strangely, it was the boarding school that saved Lise. She was desperately lonely at first, but then she pulled herself together and started to make friends. The other girls at the school were curious about her, and most of them were friendly. Lise was blonde and very pretty; her clothes were different, her accent was different and the Holbrook name was known from coast to coast. These things helped her to make friends, and she finally got over her grief and grew into a cool, reserved, well-balanced young woman.

It was at school too, that she realised her acting ambitions. She found that she loved donning the protective mantle of a character in a play. It was something she could hide behind and she was good at it. In consequence, when she left the college and moved back to San Francisco, she knew exactly what she wanted to do. She wanted to train as a professional actress.

Mason objected strongly. As far as he was concerned, she had two choices. She either continued her education, or she got married, preferably the latter and preferably to someone hand-picked by him.

'Jack might as well be dead,' he told her, his face harsh. 'There's nobody to carry on the business. You're my only hope, Lise, and I want an heir.'

She had protested strongly, suggesting Meredith as

the mother of his heir, but Mason had snorted. 'That girl is a damned half-wit, just like her mother!'

He had crushed Lise, making her aware of what she owed him—for taking her in, for educating her. He was ruthless and persuasive, used to people obeying his every wish, his standards impossibly high. But she respected him, in a frightened sort of way. She couldn't decide whether or not she loved him. He was too hard, too cold, and he never showed her any particular affection.

She decided to shelve her plans for drama school for six months. Perhaps she could persuade him in that time, bring him round to her way of thinking, although she made it very clear that she wouldn't let him push her into marriage for his own convenience.

Mason had laughed, clearly delighted, sure he had won, and Lise found herself flung head first into a hectic social life. Mason had always done a lot of entertaining at the apartment and now it seemed to be dinner party after dinner party, as he introduced Lise into the 'right' social circle.

He sent her to New York with Nancy, where a new wardrobe of wildly expensive designer clothes was bought for her, despite her protests.

'Look at your clothes. God, they're appalling!' Mason said repressively when she argued. 'You've got to look good, you've got to make the best of yourself. Everybody appreciates a beautiful woman, especially around the dinner table. So, do it for me, baby, please?'

Lise had given in under his bombarding persuasion. It didn't really matter to her what she wore at his parties. He was so obviously proud of her. It was nice to be able to please him so easily.

The men he introduced her to, though, left her cold.

She had never met a man who made her heart beat faster, and the smooth, confident businessmen Mason persistently tried to pair her off with found her cool and uninterested.

She tried to please her grandfather by smiling and being polite, but it wasn't easy, until, one night, she met Paul Lianos.

They were introduced by Mason, smiling broadly as he presented Lise.

'He's important,' Mason whispered in her ear before he left them alone together. 'For God's sake be nice to him. I think you'll have a lot in common.'

Paul Lianos was the one, Lise realised as she smiled politely, feeling shocked inside. Mason was hoping for wedding bells, and he was going to push her as hard as he had to to get what he wanted. She had looked at Paul Lianos for the first time then, and saw that he was different from the rest. He was tall and slim, in his early thirties, very sure of himself, very good-looking.

Lise had grabbed another glass of champagne from a passing waiter, and laughed as Paul Lianos charmed her with his clever, amusing conversation.

She had been wearing a grey silk dress, she remembered, that evening. She still remembered every detail. She had thrown that dress away later, stuffing it into the dustbin, hating it.

As she drank her champagne, she began to feel lightheaded. As soon as she finished it, Paul Lianos handed her another glass.

They danced, and she stared up into his handsome face, entranced, attracted to him as she had never been attracted to a man before. He was elegant and sophisticated and rather sexy and he flattered her with his smile. Lise had felt her heart beating faster as the hours flew past. Perhaps this was love. Perhaps he was feeling it too, she thought mistily, not realising his intentions until he cleverly manoeuvred her into the quiet emptiness of Mason's study.

Thinking about it now, she covered her face with her hands, unable to stop shaking. She had been so naïve, such a fool. She remembered that Mason had watched them go, smiling approvingly. How could he, she had thought later, *how could he*?

In the darkness, she had not recognised the lust in Paul Lianos' eyes. She had melted into his arms, wanting his kiss, lifting her mouth drowsily, only struggling when he tried to pull off her dress.

'No!' She had pulled away, frightened, suddenly feeling panic. He was going too fast for her, and his hands were rough, uncaring.

'Don't play games with me,' he said thickly, tearing her dress in his horrible eagerness. 'You've been asking for this all night.'

Lise hadn't been playing games. She had been really frightened, not knowing what she had done wrong.

'I don't want to——' she had whispered shakily, but Paul Lianos had ignored her.

'Your grandfather handed you to me on a plate,' he had told her, his charming smile gone, his voice savage, his face cruel. 'And I don't like girls who tease.'

He had bruised her body and left her feeling dirty and soiled. She'd cried out, fighting with all her strength, but he had clamped his hand over her mouth, using excessive violence, hurting her. Lise had never even imagined such brutality; the whole scene was like a nightmare. By sheer chance she had managed to catch him off balance for a second, and got away from him before it was too late. He had called her some terribly insulting names as she fled, threatening that if she so much as breathed a word, she would be very, very sorry. He would see to that personally.

Lise had rushed to her bedroom, locked herself in and stayed there, hardly able to believe what had happened to her. It had affected her deeply, coming at the time when she was just stepping out into the world. It had shattered her trust in men. Her own stupid innocence had trapped her with a man who had wanted nothing more than a quick and easy one-night stand. And she had thought she might be falling in love with him!

Humiliation had flayed her. She had hated him then, and hated herself for her own stupidity. Her behaviour had obviously been at fault; Paul Lianos had thought she was offering what he wanted. Her own image had confused her. Paul Lianos had stolen her self-confidence and her self-respect. Had she led him on?

With the ground pulled from under her feet, Lise had decided there and then that she would never let another man near enough to hurt her. She would be cool and wary, she would build a huge wall around herself for protection. Nobody would get through. Not ever. One night of this pain, this doubt, was enough to last her a lifetime.

The following day she had tried to tell Mason about it, but had found that she couldn't. Her own fear and the fact of his obvious liking for Paul Lianos kept her silent, but she wasn't prepared to attend Mason's parties any more.

Against all his wishes, she applied for, and got, a place at a drama school in London. She moved back to her native land, prepared to struggle on her own rather than live the charade Mason wanted for her. He hit the roof when she told him she was leaving. He threatened to cut her off without a penny, unable to understand her motives—but Lise was unshakeable. She had to get away, and acting was what she wanted to do more than anything in the world. Her only regret was that she and her grandfather had parted on such bad terms. He didn't forgive easily, and he turned his back without a qualm on those who disappointed or failed him.

She still cared that she had disappointed him, and it hurt that she hadn't heard from him in three years. She wrote occasionally, never forgetting his birthday or Christmas, but it was disheartening never to receive a reply.

Now she slid out of bed, feeling restless, and pulled on a silk wrap. There was no point in going over and over the same old ground. When she had saved up enough money, she would fly over to San Francisco and try to make it up with Mason. If she scrimped and saved every penny, it wouldn't take so long. In the meantime, though, she would have to get a job as soon as possible.

In the tiny kitchen, she switched on the kettle and made herself a pot of tea, then wandered into the lounge in bare feet and curled up in a chair by the window. In another half-hour it would be dawn. The streets below were deserted. She felt suddenly lonely, then angry at the feeling because she was used to being alone.

Jordon Hayes' dark face rose up in her mind's eye, and her mouth trembled. She had made a fool of herself in front of him, she felt sure. Those clear grey eyes had seemed to penetrate every barrier she protected herself with. What had he seen when he looked at her? He was a clever, disturbing man, and she tried to push him out of her mind, leaning her head back and closing her eyes . . .

She was woken by the sound of the doorbell buzzing persistently. She looked at the clock on the mantelpiece with dazed eyes. It was late—ten-thirty—she must have fallen asleep in the chair. She stood up, pushing her tousled hair from her eyes, wincing as she straightened her cramped spine. The doorbell was still ringing, and pursing her lips, she pulled the belt of her wrap tight and padded out of her flat. She pulled open the front door, ready to reprimand the caller for his or her persistent finger on the bell, but froze into immobility as she saw Jordon Hayes on the doorstep.

Her heart seemed to stop for a split second before pounding heavily back to life. She put her hand up to her throat, tightly gathering up the lapels of the silk wrap. He was staring at her, a faint smile touching the corners of his mouth.

'What on earth are you doing here?' she demanded, her green eyes very cold.

He didn't answer. His dark glance moved over her very slowly, from the tousled softness of her hair down over the curved body almost visible beneath her nightclothes, to her small bare feet.

'So this is what you look like when you've just got out of bed,' he said softly, his voice deep.

'What?' Lise glared at him, hot colour sweeping up over her face, her knuckles gleaming white with tension where she clutched her wrap.

'I had wondered,' he said mockingly.

The sunlight gleamed in the blackness of his hair, and Lise stared at him. 'What do you want?' she asked, but her voice was less sure, less cold.

'Let me in,' he said expressionlessly. 'Unless you want to attract even more attention than we're attracting already.'

Lise dragged her eyes from his hard face and saw curtains twitching nosily in the house across the road. A crowd of young boys had already gathered around the low black Ferrari parked at the kerb, and were watching the altercation between Lise and Jordon with curious eyes.

With a defeated sigh, she held open the door, walking quickly into her flat, leaving him to follow. He came in behind her, walking into the room with silent, cat-like grace.

Trembling, Lise put the width of the room between them, watching him with wide green eyes. He seemed to fill the small flat with his powerful masculine presence. The dinner-jacket was gone. He wore tight faded jeans that clung to his lean hips and muscular thighs, and a dark shirt, open at the neck to reveal the tanned column of his throat and the beginnings of the fine dark hair that matted his chest. He looked hard and strong and he was watching her through narrowed eyes.

Lise felt the tension between them, the awareness that was filling the room.

'Why have you come?' she demanded shakily.

'You know why,' he replied with quiet intensity, his eyes holding her wide glance effortlessly.

'No, I don't,' she lied, denying him, still confused. 'And I think you should go.'

'Aren't you going to offer me some coffee?' he asked calmly.

'No.' She wanted him to go. She felt deeply disturbed, her customary coolness long gone.

'Black. No sugar,' he drawled, ignoring her, moving, glancing around the room. She had decorated the place herself when she moved in. It was a high-ceilinged room, the walls cream, lined with bookshelves that held her books, framed photographs and ornaments. The furniture was all second-hand, the shabby chairs covered with bright paisley shawls. It was comfortable and cheerful, and it reflected Lise's cool, careful style.

Jordon had his back to her now, and she stared at his wide muscular shoulders as he glanced through her books; something inside her shivered.

She walked stiffly into the kitchen, anger rising as she spooned ground coffee into the battered percolator. Who did he think he was, barging into her flat like this? Why was he here? 'You know why,' he had said, and beneath the train of her conscious thought, she did. Something deep inside her was responding to him, straining towards him—despite everything she knew of men, despite every lesson learned in the hardest way. He had been in her mind since she first set eyes on him last night. He was haunting her subconscious.

She glanced down and saw the flimsy silk of her nightdress. She must get dressed. To be half naked put her at a disadvantage with him, and she had never before felt so aware of her own body.

She pulled two cups off the shelf, slamming them on to a tray, then, turning to go and dress, she found him leaning indolently against the door jamb, watching her.

'The coffee will be ready in a moment,' she told him acidly.

His mouth tightened at her deliberate rudeness. 'I'm glad to see that you're at least doing what you're told,' he drawled lazily.

Lise stiffened with outrage. 'If you're so desperate for a cup of coffee, why don't you buy one at a café? I hear you're filthy rich.'

Jordon straightened, flexing his powerful shoulder muscles. 'I came here to see you,' he asserted softly. 'To make sure you were okay after last night.'

Lise felt her mouth drying at something in his voice, something deep and intent and inevitable.

'Excuse me, she said coldly. 'I want to get dressed.'

She took a tentative step forward, but he was blocking her escape and he didn't move. The grey eyes narrowed on her face. 'I like you just as you are,' he teased, laughter in his voice.

'Get out of my way.' The words shook a little, but her eyes were ice-cold and dismissive.

Jordon shook his head. 'Your manners are appalling,' he said with infuriating calm, but his mouth was hard and she got the impression that he was controlling his temper with difficulty.

'I hope you're not offering any lessons,' she retorted scathingly.

He smiled. 'Don't tempt me.'

The threat was there. Lise heard it, her body responding involuntarily. She put up her hand to touch her face, and winced as her fingers encountered the bruising along her jaw. Amazingly, she had forgotten all about that.

Jordon noted her pain, moved, towering over her. He tilted up her chin with one long finger. 'Have you put anything on that?'

He was so close she could feel the clean coolness of his breath against her flushed cheeks.

'I'm fine,' she said through her teeth. Jordon shook his head.

'On the contrary, Lise, you're as cold as ice.' His fingers traced the soft, vulnerable line of her jaw. 'Why, I wonder? What dark secrets are frozen away behind those beautiful green eyes?'

Lise trembled violently beneath his touch. New feelings ran through her like fire. She had never felt like this before. Jordon Hayes possessed a sexual magnetism that left her feeling devastated, off balance and totally confused.

'Let me go!' she said, ice cracking in her voice.

'No.' He bit the word out, paused, then smiled sardonically. 'I'm going to crack that wall of ice, Lise, I'm giving you that promise now.'

Shaken, she looked up into the narrowed, expressionless depths of his eyes. 'You frighten me,' she whispered.

'I want you,' he replied, holding her glance.

The shock of the coolly spoken words held her rigid. She didn't know how to react. No man had got this close to her before—but then she hadn't met anybody like Jordon Hayes before. There was a ruthless persistence in his eyes that scared the living daylights out of her. She had to pull herself together, retaliate somehow, because in her heart she knew he had the power to destroy her if she let him too near. She twisted her head out of his grasp, surprised when his hand dropped, letting her go easily.

'You're wasting your time, Mr Hayes,' she said, with as much coolness as she could muster. 'I'm afraid the feeling is definitely not reciprocated.'

She turned away, her inside twisted as tight as wire, her heart beating so fast she thought it would suffocate her. Aware that he was watching her every movement, she unplugged the percolator and picked it up, her hands shaking so much that the cups rattled alarmingly.

Without a word, Jordon took the tray from her trembling fingers and carried it into the lounge. He poured coffee for them both, easily, taking charge.

Lise watched his hands, so strong and sure. She felt as though she was on the edge of a precipice. The smallest of moves could send her hurtling into the unknown darkness.

As he handed her the cup of steaming liquid, she looked up and found him staring at her. Their eyes held, his clear and watchful, hers wide and frightened. 'Is there somebody else?' he asked. 'That guy you were dancing with last night?'

'Ashley?' Lise seized on that, smiling with relief, wanting him to misunderstand. 'I don't think that's any of your business.'

'Boy-friend?' His voice was still calm but his mouth was hard, his eyes curiously blank.

'Yes,' lied Lise triumphantly. 'I might marry him.'

Jordon moved, and she shot to her feet, giving away her nervousness.

'You don't give a damn about him,' he said softly, walking towards her.

'That's ridiculous!' Lise backed away until she found herself trapped against the smooth wall. 'You know nothing——'

'I know that you were keeping him on his knees, freezing him off with those wide green eyes whenever he got too close. He's no match for you, Lise, and you know it.'

He towered over her, advancing deliberately, his words sardonic.

'And I suppose you think you are?' she demanded scathingly.

He smiled, placing his hands on the wall at either side of her, trapping her.

'Shall I show you?' he asked, watching her.

The breath caught in her throat. Her body felt stiff with an agony of tension. 'Don't touch me,' she whispered through dry lips, feeling the cold wall against the skin of her back.

Jordon was silent for a moment, his eyes moving over her pale face, coming to rest on the vulnerable softness of her mouth. 'Don't be so provocative, then,' he said finally, half smiling.

'There are other people in this house,' she managed jerkily. 'If I scream, someone will come running.'

Jordon laughed. 'And are you going to scream?'

'Damn you, let me go!' Aware of the taunt, aware of the turmoil of emotion churning inside her, she was deliberately goading him, she knew that. Yet she also knew that she didn't want him to touch her. If he did . . .

'You've got a lot to learn,' said Jordan coolly. 'The first lesson being that I give orders, I don't take them.'

He moved so that their bodies touched. Lise could feel the hardness of his thighs brushing hers, and her pulse speeded dizzily. She stared up helplessly into his strong, lean face. 'Don't,' she whispered, in the grip of emotions so fierce she was hardly aware of what she was saying. 'Jordon, please——'

But it was too late. He lowered his head slowly, his hard, beautifully moulded mouth touching hers briefly, gently, before forcing her lips apart with a savage, bruising kiss.

Lise struggled wildly for a moment, until his hands came up to frame her face, holding her still, leaving her totally at his mercy.

Memories of Paul Lianos filled her mind. Her hands clenched at her sides, and her body stiffened in sudden uncontrollable panic. She thought she was going to die. She couldn't breathe.

Jordon, sensing her fear, though he could not know the reason for it, lifted his mouth from hers, sliding his lips tenderly along the soft white line of her throat. His hands stroked gently through her tousled silver hair, stilling her, calming her.

Lise stood trembling violently, head back, eyes closed. His mouth was like fire. He wasn't Paul Lianos. He was Jordon Hayes. He was imprinted on her mind, his image burning behind her eyelids. As his mouth caressed the pulse that beat frantically in her throat, she knew with fierce clarity that she would never, ever confuse him with any other man.

The memories of Paul Lianos' brutality faded as though they had never existed. An unknown heat coursed through her body, her blood ran hot and quick. It blotted out everything. There was nothing in her body or her mind except the knowledge of Jordon's lovemaking. His mouth traced the fragile bones of her shoulders, making her shudder violently, uncontrollably.

Jordon raised his head, looking down into her face with half-closed, glittering eyes. Their bodies were still touching.

Lise opened her own eyes, looking helplessly up at him, and Jordon drew breath raggedly as he read her expression.

In heavy silence he caught her hands and placed them around his neck, his own hands coming to rest possessively at her waist. Lise didn't protest. Her body was quickening with the passion he was arousing in her.

'Lise,' he murmured her name huskily before bending his head, finding her mouth again with a deep, drugging kiss.

All anger was gone. He showed her his hunger, his desire. Their mouths clung, hers parting, her response as violent as it was unbidden.

Jordon's hands slid up her body to cup her breasts. Lise moaned into his throat, her fingers clenching in the thick darkness of his hair. Jordon's body tensed, he pulled her closer into the circle of his arms. Hardly aware of what she was doing, she leant against him, her bones melting, needing his support. The touch of his strong mouth made her burn for more.

He was still kissing her, exploring the softness of her lips with an intimacy she had never experienced before. His long fingers moved, gently sliding the silk wrap from her shoulders, flicking aside the thin straps of her nightdress so that it fell to her waist, exposing the fullness of her naked breasts. His mouth followed the path laid bare by his hands, his cool lips sliding erotically over her skin. He kissed the scented hollow between her breasts and his mouth was gentle, lips moving, his tongue lazily touching her stiffening, aching nipples, until Lise groaned, digging her fingers convulsively into the unyielding muscles of his shoulders.

Then she felt him stiffen; he lifted his head, his face set in harsh lines of self-control. He pulled the nightdress up over her swollen breasts, sliding the straps on to her bare shoulders, releasing her almost abruptly.

Lise frowned as he left her, clutching at the wall for support, her legs unwilling to hold her up. Drowsily she opened her eyes. Jordon was staring into her face, his expression intent as he noted the bruised softness of her lips, the dark desire lingering in her eyes.

The icy façade was cracked wide open, revealing the vulnerable woman within. Lise looked at him, unable to hide a thing in the aftermath of their exchanged passion.

'God, Lise, you're so beautiful,' he said, smiling, his

face deeply sensual. But his words broke the spell. She turned away, bitter tears scalding her eyes. What had she given away in his arms? Her body was still aching, unsatisfied, frustrated. She pulled her wrap tightly around her, unable to look at him. No man had touched her like that before. She had wanted him, still wanted him. The knowledge was alien, shattering. She couldn't cope with it.

'Please go,' she whispered, staring out of the window to the street, where life was going on as usual, people walking past, children playing. She felt him move. He came to stand beside her.

'Who was he?' he asked quietly.

His perception didn't surprise her, but she had no intention of telling him anything. She had already revealed far too much of herself. She was silent.

'Lise?' He turned her to face him and she was shocked by the anger she saw in his eyes. 'Who was he?' he asked again.

Her face closed. 'If you've got what you came for, I'd like you to go,' she muttered, under her breath.

She felt his fingers tightening on her shoulders, knowing with strange satisfaction that the movement was involuntary.

'You know what I want,' he said softly. 'And you know damn well that neither of us is satisfied.'

Hot colour swept over Lise's face. He was too direct, too honest. She fought the urge to hit him, instinctively knowing that in any battle with him she would come off worst.

'I . . . Oh, just leave me alone!' She was lost for words, which was very unusual.

'Have dinner with me tonight,' he said, looking at her.

Panic showed in her eyes. She didn't want this

earth-shattering awareness of him; it scared her. She sensed his power, the ruthlessness behind the cool charm, and backed away. Her impulse was to run and hide.

'I can't,' she replied honestly. 'I already have plans.'

Jordon's eyes narrowed. 'Who?'

'Mind your own business!' she shot back defiantly.

His smile was harsh. 'Ashley?'

'No.' Something forced her to answer honestly, though she hated doing it.

'Tomorrow, then,' he said implacably.

Lise swung her head round in agitation. 'Why?' she asked shakily.

'I want to get to know you,' he replied with devastating honesty. 'I've seen the woman inside the block of ice and you intrigue me.'

'I don't want to have dinner with you—I don't want to see you again. Can't you understand that?' Her voice was too high.

Jordon's mouth tightened. 'I can understand it, but I can't accept it. I'll pick you up at eight o'clock tomorrow.' His voice was even, brooking no argument.

'I won't be here,' Lise said fiercely.

'You will.' The grey eyes held hers. She felt the sheer force of his will, her lashes sweeping down to hide her submission.

'Damn you,' she whispered, shaking. 'I hate you, do you hear me? *I hate you*!'

Jordon smiled. 'You little liar,' he murmured, reaching out to touch her loose hair.

She flinched away, acknowledging the painful truth of his words. Hate was far too tame a word for what she was feeling now. Her emotions were reeling. The ground that had been so solid beneath her feet was shifting, cracking wide open.

Nobody had breached the barriers she had set up around herself. Until now. Jordon Hayes had walked into her life and knocked down those barricades within five minutes of their meeting. He had left her raw and exposed, and she needed some time to lick her wounds, to patch herself together again.

Jordon moved towards the door, tall and strong and powerful. 'Eight, tomorrow!' he reminded her with a smile.

'Jordon——' She stopped him as he opened the door, not knowing why she was calling him back, only knowing that she didn't want him to go. She didn't want to be alone.

He turned, watching her.

'I ... well, I ...' Her confusion showed in her stricken eyes, and he sighed.

'Lise, for God's sake, stop looking at me like that,' he groaned. In two long strides he covered the ground between them, his hands closing on her shoulders, as he bent to brush her mouth with his own.

'Tomorrow,' he said softly against her lips, then he was gone, leaving her shaken and very, very worried.

CHAPTER THREE

LISE woke early the following morning, stretching languidly as she remembered her vivid dreams of Jordon Hayes.

She couldn't stop thinking about him; that hard masculine face was in her mind all the time.

Stop it, she told herself, don't get involved with him. He'll only hurt you—you know that. But as she sat in her tiny kitchen drinking coffee, her thoughts drifted back. She knew hardly anything about him, she realised, only what Jerri had told her: merchant banker, patron of the theatre. God, she must stop thinking about him!

She washed her coffee cup, forcing herself to think straight. She remembered how it had felt when he touched her, when he kissed her. She had made a fool of herself, and outraged pride stiffened her spine. If he thought he could bully her into going out to dinner with him tonight, he could think again.

She telephoned her agent before noon; he was always in his office before lunch. He had nothing for her. He would ring her at the end of the week, he promised, but Lise had the feeling he was putting her off, friendly and sympathetic though he sounded. Either way, she would have to get some sort of a job, and soon. Since leaving drama school she had done just about every job imaginable, between parts. Waitressing, washing up, shop work, child-minding. She would start asking around. The rent on the flat was due in two weeks' time and she hardly had a penny saved. Suddenly the outlook was not particularly bright, and she picked up yesterday's newspaper, scanning the job columns, feeling an unusual depression settling over her.

She was still feeling pretty miserable when Jerri called late in the afternoon. The older girl whirled into the flat, bright and cheerful in a summery pastel dress and jacket.

'I'm just on my way to the dry-cleaners,' she announced as she sat down, 'and I thought I'd pick up that black dress.'

Lise retrieved it from her bedroom. 'Sorry,' she said, smiling as she handed it over 'I meant to have it cleaned myself and drop it over to you, but I didn't get round to it. I'll give you the money.'

'Don't be silly.' Jerri eyed her curiously. 'Darling, what on earth have you done to your face?'

'Oh, that?' Lise explained briefly, not mentioning Jordon Hayes.

Jerri listened, wide-eyed. 'Drunks!' she said expressively. 'They make me sick. You *are* all right?'

Lise nodded. 'Yes—there was no real damage done. Would you like some tea?'

'A cup of coffee would be lovely.' Jerri sighed as though parched.

Lise switched on the percolator, her black mood lifting a little. Jerri was always good company; she could make anybody laugh with her sharp wit. And she was always so elegant. Lise looked down at her old jeans and pastel pink sweatshirt and grimaced, suddenly dissatisfied with herself.

'Nick wants *both* his suits cleaned,' Jerri was saying as she slipped off her bright cotton jacket and smoothed down her black hair. 'He's having lunch with a backer next week. Would you believe, I'm *not* invited, even though I could get time off rehearsals? He can be such a pig!'

Lise laughed as she carried in the tray. 'When do rehearsals start?' she asked, half enviously.

'Monday,' groaned Jerri. 'I was hoping we could get away for a long weekend, but Nick's invited some people round on Sunday, so that's gone by the board.'

Hearing Jerri talking about her husband with that careless intimacy and obvious affection only served to emphasise Lise's strange loneliness. She didn't know where it had come from. She had been living alone for three years now; the way she had been brought up had made her tough and self-sufficient. She never felt lonely, never felt that indefinable yearning inside her. But she felt it now. She'd been feeling it all day: a longing, a dissatisfaction with the way her life was.

'Sorry, what did you say?' Deep in thought, she had missed what Jerri was talking about.

'Nick says she's broken her ankle. Janet Nairn,' Jerri repeated patiently. 'Skiing, or something like that. I suppose it couldn't be skiing at this time of the year. Anyway, it's only a small part, but Joe doesn't want to start rehearsals until he's got someone—you know what he's like, so stuffy and proper. I can get you an audition if you like. You haven't got anything else lined up, have you?'

Lise laughed delightedly. 'I've been looking through the situations vacant,' she said, pointing at the discarded newspaper.

She could hardly believe her luck. She already knew the play. As Jerri said, it was only a small part, but she was going to jump at the chance, grab it with both hands. It would be so nice to work with Jerri again, too.

'Wonderful! I'll phone Joe tonight.' Jerri held out

her cup for more coffee. 'We'll be able to share a dressing-room again!'

'I haven't got the part yet,' Lise reminded her.

'I bet you will, though, darling; look at your reviews! And I'll sing your praises to Joe when I speak to him. It's in the bag!'

Lise couldn't help laughing. Jerri's enthusiasm was infectious, and the thought of being in work again so soon—if she passed the audition—made her heart sing.

'I suppose you've heard the latest gossip,' said Jerri with the air of a conspirator, leaning back in her seat, sipping her fresh coffee.

'What gossip?' Lise hadn't heard anything. For the past couple of days she had been totally wrapped up in her own problems.

'Caroline and Ash,' pronounced Jerri mysteriously, eyes dancing.

'Tell!' Lise curled her legs under her.

'They left the club together after the party, you know? And Penny phoned me this morning. She'd been trying to get in touch with Caroline. I suggested she tried Ashley's place. I was half joking, or maybe just being bitchy.' Jerri laughed. 'Anyway, she did, and Caroline was there! It's possibly the romance of the year!'

Lise smiled. She was glad. She and Caroline had never been friends, but perhaps that had been because of Ash. Lise was happy that she'd finally got what she so obviously wanted.

'That's good news.'

'You don't mind?' asked Jerri curiously.

'Why should I?' Lise's surprise was genuine.

'Come on, Ash followed you around like a tame dog! I thought——'

'Well, you thought wrong,' Lise cut in firmly. 'I never encouraged him. In fact, with Caroline giving me daggers every time I so much as looked at him, I wouldn't have dared even if I *had* fancied him.'

'Oh, I see.' Jerri digested this, her mouth curved in a sweet smile. 'And I suppose you've got bigger fish to fry now, anyway.'

'I don't know what you mean!' Although she protested, Lise felt the betraying flush of colour in her cheeks. Jerri saw it too and pounced on it.

'Oh, yes, you do! Jordon Hayes! Somebody told me you left the club with him.'

'I . . . Well . . . yes, he gave me a lift home,' admitted Lise reluctantly; she had to smile at the avid curiosity in Jerri's eyes.

'And?'

'And he dropped round yesterday.' She felt her face getting hotter and hotter. Why was she being so secretive? Jerri would suspect the worst, she knew, but she just couldn't bring herself to talk easily about Jordon Hayes. Her reaction to him embarrassed her. She, who was always so calm and in control. She, who could freeze a man's advances without giving him a second thought. It was ridiculous.

'Really?' Jerri's eyes had that faraway, envious look. 'God, you lucky thing! When are you seeing him again?'

Lise shrugged, looking away. 'He asked me to have dinner with him tonight, but I said no.'

'You said . . . Lise, are you out of your mind?' Jerri sat up straight, her face filled with horror.

'I don't want to get involved with him,' said Lise defensively. 'He's . . .' She paused, unable to frame her thoughts.

'What?' Jerri prompted. 'Too sexy? Too rich? Most

women would give their right arm for a dinner invitation from Jordon Hayes!'

'Not me.' Lise's mouth was a straight stubborn line, and she had the feeling that she was lying.

'He could do a hell of a lot for your career,' said Jerri softly.

'I'd never do that,' Lise replied, frowning. 'It's immoral.'

'I know you wouldn't.' The older girl laughed at Lise's outraged expression. 'You're so old-fashioned.'

'Am I?' Perhaps she was; she'd never really thought about it. 'Old-fashioned or not, that's a thing I'll never do. It *is* wrong to use people like that.'

Jerri lit a cigarette with careless grace. 'I agree with you, darling, but you can't deny that it is how a lot of people get on. Although I doubt that a man like Jordon Hayes would let himself be used in any way at all.'

Lise flushed, picturing those hard, tanned features in her mind. Jerri was right: Jordon was not the sort of man people used. He commanded far too much respect.

'I don't know what sort of man he is,' she thought aloud.

'Is it important?' asked Jerri, laughing. 'I mean, with all that sex appeal, I could very easily be blinded to the man underneath.'

Lise thought for a moment. 'Yes, it is important. I don't know a thing about him.'

'What's to know? He's a banker. He's American. The newspapers chase him all over the world. He's big news, and his women are always beautiful, intelligent and talented. If I were you, I'd count myself lucky to be among that élite group. And if you're *still* worried, you can find out what sort of man he is over dinner!'

Jerri glanced at her watch. 'I'll have to fly if I want to catch the cleaners. What are you going to wear tonight?'

Lise shrugged. 'I haven't decided whether or not I'm going yet.'

Jerri laughed. 'Go! And I'll ring you tomorrow for all the news.'

Later, as Lise walked back to the flat, her arms full of shopping, she reflected on what Jerri had said. If she was seen around with Jordon, would people think she was trying to further her career? Would *he* think that? Would people assume she was sleeping with him? Did she really care what anybody thought? Her mind ran round in circles; she was making excuses. She wanted to have dinner with him, but she was frightened. She had no protection against him.

As she turned the corner into her street, she didn't hear the voice calling her name, and she jumped as a hand touched her shoulder, one of her bags slipping from her hand. It hit the floor with a crack, its contents rolling out on to the pavement.

'Sorry!' Shaun Barnett's face smiled into hers as he bent to re-pack and retrieve the dropped bag 'I didn't mean to startle you.'

'I was miles away,' Lise admitted, glad to see him. Shaun lived in the flat above hers; he had helped her with her furniture when she moved in. He worked for an advertising agency in the City. He was young and good-looking, with soft blond hair that fell across his forehead. Ever since they met, he had asked her out from time to time. Lise had always found an excuse to put him off.

She liked him a lot, he was charming and amusing, yet she knew with some sixth sense that his feelings could be much stronger than her own. If she gave in and went out with him, she doubted that they would remain friends.

He straightened, her shopping tucked under his arm. 'Let me take that.' He indicated her other bag.

'That's very gallant of you.' It was a relief; her arms were aching. 'Finished for the day?' she asked brightly.

'Mmm.' He glanced at her, his blue eyes narrowed against the glare of the sun. 'How about you? Found anything yet?'

She told him about the part in the play Jerri was working in. 'She's going to try and get me an audition.'

'That's great!' Shaun sounded genuinely pleased.

They reached the flat, and Lise opened the front door, holding it wide. He walked through. 'Do you want this stuff in the kitchen?'

'Yes, please. Tea?'

'Sure. Today has been particularly harrowing.' They chatted idly and drank tea. Shaun made her laugh with scandalous stories about the company whose account he was working on at present, and Lise felt her anxiety draining away. She spent too much time on her own, she decided. She let little problems grow out of all proportion. Shaun's company brought her back to reality. The room seemed full of sunshine, even though it was early evening. Everything was fine.

'Let's go out for a meal tonight,' Shaun suggested some time later. 'I'm starving.'

Lise shook her head. 'I hadn't really planned on going out tonight,' she said apologetically. She wanted to keep a low profile. She was in hiding.

'Okay.' He took her refusal lightly, easily. 'I could get us something from the Chinese take-away round the corner?'

She smiled, glad of his understanding. 'That would

be nice.' she agreed cautiously.

'What would you like?' He stared at her, his eyes suddenly dark.

'I don't know. You choose.' She felt unable to make even the smallest decision. Eight o'clock was fast approaching and her stomach was coiled with nerves. She felt utterly ashamed of herself as well. Was she letting Shaun stay because she needed someone with her when she told Jordon Hayes that she had no intention of having dinner with him?

'But I want to pay for my own,' she insisted firmly.

'Oh, no, I want to treat you.' His smile was disarming. 'You've never let me buy you dinner.'

The sound of the doorbell broke into their lighthearted wrangling. Lise froze, her face paling.

'That's your doorbell,' Shaun laughed when she made no move to answer it.

Trembling, she walked to the door and out into the hall, taking a deep, shaking breath as she pulled open the heavy front door. Jordan Hayes stood outside, tall, dark and powerful in a beautifully tailored suit that seemed to emphasise the muscular strength of his body.

'Hello Lise,' he said quietly, his grey eyes holding hers.

'Hello.' She heard her own voice as though from miles away, her breath coming quickly and strangely. 'I . . . I wasn't expecting you,' she lied, to hide her confusion.

'It's eight o'clock,' he said with calm amusement. 'Had you forgotten?'

He knew that she hadn't. Her confusion revealed everything. 'It wasn't a definite arrangement,' she retorted, using defiance as her only weapon.

'Sure it was.' He smiled, and watching that smile

from beneath her lashes, Lise felt something twisting painfully inside her. Frightened suddenly, she was aware of his indomitable will, his self-assurance and the strength beneath his charm.

'Are you ready?' he asked patiently. His dark glance slid over her, taking in her loose pink shirt and faded jeans, her face bare of make-up and her blonde hair pulled back into a tight ponytail. Aware of what a sight she must look compared to the sophisticated woman at the nightclub, Lise flushed hotly under his gaze, realising with a pang of shock that she *wanted* to look good for him. She wanted to look her best. The patient note she imagined she heard in his voice made her teeth snap together.

'Ready?' she echoed blankly. 'I told you yesterday, Mr Hayes, that I had no intention of having dinner with you tonight, and I meant it. I'm afraid I've made other plans.'

She moved to close the front door in his face, but he was too fast for her, too strong. Before she realised it, he was in the hall, striding into her flat. Furiously, she followed, intending to throw him out bodily if she had to.

Shaun jumped to his feet as they entered the lounge, his face flushing with nervous guilt as though he had been caught doing something wrong.

He's afraid, Lise realised with sad surprise, although when she looked at Jordon she knew why. His face was set, his eyes as cold as ice. Every line of his body threatened, though he stood very still.

Shaun got to his feet, his feeling of intimidation clear, though he obviously recognised the man in front of him. 'Shaun Barnett,' he introduced himself with an uneasy smile. 'I'm pleased to meet you, Mr Hayes.'

Jordon didn't take the proffered hand, he merely

inclined his dark head in acknowledgement. The steel-grey eyes focused coldly on Lise. 'Get ready,' he told her expressionlessly.

Shaun took a step towards the door. He half-smiled at Lise, his face red. 'I didn't realise you had a date for this evening.' He tried to keep the reproach out of his voice.

Lise shrugged. 'I don't,' she bit out, so angry that she hardly trusted herself to speak.

'You're leaving?' Jordon cut in with a cold smile.

Shaun nodded, muttering something under his breath before shooting through the door like a scalded cat. Lise came to her senses as the door slammed shut.

'Shaun——' She followed him out into the hall. 'I'm so sorry,' she said, feeling awful, knowing that she had no words to put it right.

'Don't apologise. It doesn't matter.'

She knew that it did; she could see the disappointment in his face. 'But I *am* sorry,' she said again, cursing her own selfishness, wishing with all her heart that she hadn't hurt him. 'Because it's all my fault—I . . .' She wanted to explain, but as their eyes met, she knew that explanations were unnecessary.

So much for all her pompous talk to Jerri about morals! Shaun was well aware that she had let him stay because she was afraid of facing Jordon on her own. Shaun wasn't strong or tough. He was no match for Jordon. She had known that, and now he knew it too.

She could see that he thought she and Jordon were involved with each other. He thought she had been using him in some bitter private battle. It was too embarrassing to contemplate.

'Forget it.' He turned away and continued climbing the stairs. 'I'll see you around.'

Lise watched him go in silence. His pride was hurt, and she hated herself. She would never be able to make it up to him.

With tears filling her eyes she marched back into her flat. Jordon was standing with his back to the window, his wide shoulders blocking out the last of the sunlight. He watched her walk towards him, his face unreadable.

'How could you?' she stormed at him through her tears. 'How could you treat him like that?'

'Like what?' he demanded crisply.

'You were unforgivably rude,' Lise sniffed. 'You made him go.'

'You wanted him to stay?' The question was calmly spoken, though his eyes probed her face.

'We were going to have a meal together,' she said fiercely, looking round for something with which to dry her eyes.

'You're having dinner with me,' Jordon reminded her, reaching into the pocket of his jacket, and handing her a clean white handkerchief.

She took it grudgingly, quelling the urge to slap his face. Her eyes felt sore and swollen; she felt a positive mess. She tried to breathe deeply, tried to control the trembling in her stomach. What was there about him that made her react so violently whenever she was with him?

'After this I wouldn't have dinner with you if you were the last man on earth!' she told him angrily.

Jordon's eyes were strangely gentle. 'Go and wash your face, and get changed,' he said quietly, yet the warning was there.

'No.' She folded her arms across her breasts, and met his eyes defiantly, her mouth a stubborn line.

He contemplated her narrowly. 'What's the matter

now? You want to talk about Shaun Barnett?'

Lise nodded. 'Why were you so rude to him?'

Jordon smiled. 'What did I say?'

'You . . .' She stopped, thinking back. What had he said? Shaun hadn't responded to words, but to something in Jordon's eyes, in his face, in the stance of his body. Jordon's very presence had been intimidating.

'Well?' His voice teased. The sudden charming smile made her senses reel.

'Oh, I don't know!' He was right, and she felt unreasonably irritated.

'Precisely. You're going to have to carry the guilt, Lise, you can't push it on to me. You deliberately placed him in the firing line. You dragged him into our private war.' He forced her to see that she was in the wrong, and to accept the blame for what she'd done.

'I know,' she whispered painfully. 'And I hate myself.'

Jordon turned away, staring out of the window. Beneath the expensive cloth of his jacket his powerful shoulders were tense.

'He's crazy about you—I suppose you know that.'

Lise didn't answer. She hadn't consciously realised it, but she knew that he was right—which made what she had done all the worse.

'How can I make it up to him?' she wondered miserably.

'He won't want your pity,' said Jordan harshly.

She stared at him. 'I suppose you think you're very clever,' she muttered acidly. He turned, laughing, looking at her in the fading light.

'I wouldn't say that,' he drawled with amusement. 'But I am hungry! Are you going to get changed or will I have to do it for you.' He took a step towards her and she shrank back. In the dim light he looked bigger, more powerful, and she didn't doubt for a second that he meant what he said.

She knew that she should reach out and turn on the light. She could reach it from where she was standing, but to do so would reveal too much, and her pride forbade her to do it.

'Don't you threaten me,' she said, trying to hold her ground. 'You can't force your way in here, and . . . and . . .'

He was moving closer as she spoke, and her mouth dried, words tailing off. Tension cracked between them like raw electricity. In the darkness Jordon's face seemed sculptured, shadowed; his eyes gleamed darkly.

'Lise,' he threatened softly, and she listened, spellbound to hear the way he said her name, so softly, and with that unfamiliar intonation that made it sound like a caress.

Don't be a fool, a little voice in her head told her, don't fall for his charm.

She looked him straight in the eye. 'Stop bullying me,' she said coldly. 'And if you don't mind, I'd like you——'

'Dammit, Lise, are you always going to fight me like this?' he cut in, losing his patience with her.

'Always?' Her green eyes widened at the implication.

'Always,' he repeated deliberately.

A terrible hot excitement fought with panic, her face reflecting her inner turmoil. They were standing only inches apart.

'No,' she denied desperately, lifting her hand as though to hit him. 'No!'

Jordon caught her wrist in his fingers before it came

near him, using his strength to pull her closer, his hard mouth touching hers with anger, with desire.

Lise groaned, her lips parting helplessly, and he began to kiss her deeply. It seemed as though she had waited for ever to feel the touch of his mouth again. She shivered and his arms came round her. He raised his mouth from hers.

'It seems to me that you have two choices,' he said huskily, his cool breath fanning her cheeks. 'Either you go and get changed for dinner, right now, or I take you to bed and make love to you until I've satisfied this ache in my inside.'

Lise's heart missed a beat. Her mouth trembled in a smile. 'I'll go and get changed,' she whispered, reaching up to touch his smooth, hard face.

He caught her hand, turning the palm to his lips, and kissing it tenderly. The brush of his mouth was very sensual, and she pulled away, shuddering, and fled to the dark sanctuary of her bedroom.

'There wasn't much to choose from in her wardrobe, she thought ruefully as she flicked through the hanging garments. Since she had left San Francisco, her clothes budget had been practically non-existent. Finally she chose a white linen dress with matching jacket. It was summery and light, yet just chic enough to pass muster at the most exclusive restaurant. She washed quickly, then made up her face with trembling hands, before catching back her hair in a stylish knot at the nape of her neck. The final touch was a pair of tiny diamond earrings that had belonged to her mother.

She looked at her reflection in the mirror and grimaced. She looked calm and collected and—ordinary. Tonight she would have liked to look beautiful.

Half smiling at her own silly thoughts, she walked out of the bedroom and back into the lounge.

Jordon was waiting for her, idly smoking a cigarette. He turned slowly, his eyes assessing her from head to foot.

'Very demure,' he commented drily. 'And quite a change from the club the other night.'

Lise shrugged. 'I'm ready.' Her voice sounded sulky. She had no intention of telling him that her finery had been borrowed; he could think what he liked.

'At last.' His voice teased her, but she didn't respond, walking out of the flat with her head held defiantly high.

The restaurant he took her to was very famous and very expensive. She knew of its reputation of course, but she had never expected to actually eat there. As they were shown to their table by a very deferential head waiter, Lise glimpsed a number of well-known faces among the smartly dressed clientele.

Jordon himself was causing something of a stir; quite a few heads were turning as they walked through the restaurant. A number of women were eyeing him openly, their attention caught by the impact of his hard good looks and powerful physique. And they were eyeing Lise as well, dismissively for the most part, after a quick look from head to toe. They probably knew to the penny how much her dress had cost, she thought, suppressing a giggle. And they were probably wondering how on earth she had managed to wangle a dinner invitation with a man like Jordon Hayes.

Their table was one of the best in the restaurant, hidden from public gaze in a discreet alcove. Crystal and silver shimmered on the white linen tablecloth;

the menu was as big as a newspaper. Lise hid behind it, her eyes skimming over the choice of delicious food, her appetite almost non-existent.

The waiters hovered solicitously and she finally chose pumpkin soup, followed by a seafood pastry with mixed salad. Jordon ordered the wine and chose smoked salmon and steak and kidney pudding with vegetables.

He smiled at Lise as the waiters vanished. 'I like to eat English food when I'm over here,' he explained.

'Well, you can't get much more English than steak and kidney pudding,' she replied, laughing.

Their eyes met and the laughter died. Her eyes dropped immediately, her face hot. She watched as Jordon tasted the wine. She watched the strong muscles contracting in his throat, as he swallowed. She watched the strength in his hands as he lifted the crystal glass to his lips. Then she looked away quickly.

The waiter filled her glass and she reached for it, sipping the bitter-sweet liquid appreciatively. It was excellent wine.

Conscious of Jordon's gaze, she asked, 'Do you spend a lot of time in England?' It was the first thing that came into her head—anything to break the silence.

'About three months every year. I have business interests over here.' He smiled, his hard face slashed with charm.

Lise nodded, trying the pumpkin soup that had been set in front of her. It was spicy and deliciously creamy, and it warmed her cold, nervous throat.

'Are you married?' she asked, suddenly shaking with fear because he might be and it hadn't occurred to her before.

He shook his head. 'I was married once. Not now.'

'What happened, a divorce?' The words were out before she realised it and she flushed with embarrassment at her own nosiness.

'She died in childbirth.' He said it levelly, calmly, as though it had never touched him.

Lise felt her heart contracting with pain.

'I'm sorry,' she said inadequately.

'Don't be. It was a long time ago.' He shrugged. 'I'm not the same person I was then.'

'What happened to the child?' she was driven to ask.

'Stillborn.' The one word was clipped, his cool eyes didn't ask for sympathy. She saw his strength, his self-sufficiency. He faced the world squarely without giving an inch.

'Did you love her?' she whispered, still caught in the tragedy.

He laughed. 'Lise, you're an incurable romantic!'

The low drawl sent shivers down her spine and brought her out of her sadness with a jolt.

'Am I?' She considered for a moment. 'No, I don't think I am, and——' her wide green eyes met his, 'you haven't answered my question. Am I prying?'

'On the contrary, I find your interest very flattering!' He raised his glass to hers, in a mocking salute. 'And to answer your question: yes, I loved her.'

Again the words were dispassionate, but a dart of emotion pierced Lise's heart. For a split second, she could imagine what it would be like to have the love of a man like Jordon. One look at him told her that he was an expert lover, gentle, possessive and strong. She bit her lip, her curiosity deeply aroused by the thought of his wife. A million questions sprang to mind. What was her name, what had she looked like? How long were they married, and most importantly, did he still mourn her loss? Was he still in love with her? She couldn't ask one of them, she realised with frustration.

'You look very serious.' His deep voice broke into her reverie, and she looked up to find him watching her.

'I was just thinking.' She pushed away her soup unfinished, wishing she could chat lightly to him, ease the tension somehow. Usually, social small-talk came easily to her but when she was with Jordon she felt tongue-tied, confused, serious. The time they spent together was too important to be wasted. He probably thought her utterly boring, she realised, with a sinking heart.

'About what?'

'Oh, about you and me,' she replied self-consciously.

His eyebrows lifted questioningly, the triumphant gleam in his eyes making her realise she had just admitted that there *was* already something between them. 'What I mean is—that I feel ridiculously shy,' she amended quickly. 'I don't know what to say, and I just wish—oh, I don't know!' She felt overwhelmed by the power of his personality.

Jordon watched the troubled movements of her hands as she spoke. She was more vulnerable than he had realised. He had cracked the wall of ice she sheltered behind, and she was unprotected. The woman he sat with now was a far cry from the cool, sexily-dressed woman he had encountered at the night club. This was the real Lise Holbrook, and somebody had hurt her pretty badly.

'It doesn't matter,' he said quietly. 'You don't have to say anything. You're not here to entertain me.'

'Aren't I? I don't know why I am here!' she said fiercely, suddenly hurt by his kindness.

'I think you do.' His smile was wicked, and she

returned it without thinking, her green eyes sparkling. He was too attractive, she thought with wonder, and she couldn't help herself responding.

The seafood dish she had ordered was delicious—prawns, mussels and baby clams in a mouthwatering sauce, nesting beneath a melting golden pastry.

As they ate, Jordon deliberately made her laugh, relaxing her, amusing her. The tension between them disappeared as he made a conscious effort to put her at ease. The wine flowed freely, and Lise found herself drinking more than she intended to. It relieved her inhibitions and allowed her to talk easily.

Jordon asked her about her career, about her life, as though every tiny detail interested him. She glossed over her time spent in San Francisco, only the faint shadowing of her eyes giving her away. He listened intently, never taking his eyes off her face. Time flew past. They sat bound in their interest in each other, almost unaware of their surroundings.

Over coffee and excellent brandy, Jordon offered her a cigarette from the gold case he extracted from his pocket. Lise took one, her eyes on his hand as he held out a gold lighter. Everything he owned was expensive, the best money could buy. She looked up at him curiously, through the thickness of her lashes.

'I think I've told you just about every boring detail about myself,' she said, a little embarrassed. 'It must be your turn now. Have you any brothers or sisters?'

'One sister. She's married and lives in Paris for most of the year.' He drew on his cigarette, exhaling smoke through his lips.

'And your parents?' Lise prompted, smiling. He was not the sort of man who told you his life story; it was like getting blood out of a stone.

He shrugged. 'Both dead. My father drank himself

into an early grave; my mother followed soon after.
He was a bastard. He used to beat her up on a regular
basis. She must have loved him, I guess; she certainly
couldn't live without him.'

Lise frowned at the sparse, brutal words. She
wanted to know more, but she didn't feel she had the
right to ask.

They left the restaurant very late. The night air was
warm and dusty, and a curious feeling of contentment
settled over Lise as she leant back her head on the
plush leather headrest. The black Ferrari was sleek
and powerful; it purred through the bright London
streets, back to her flat.

'Tired?' Jordan turned his dark head, his eyes
glittering, as he looked at her.

'Exhausted,' she replied, closing her eyes. 'I drank
far too much tonight, and I didn't sleep very well last
night.'

She looked at his hard profile as he smiled, and
wondered what she had given away by that admission.

When the car slid to a halt outside her flat, she
fumbled in her handbag for her keys.

'It was a lovely meal,' she said, keeping her head
down to hide her flushed cheeks. 'Thank you.'

Jordon reached for her in silence, gently tilting up
her face so that she was forced to look at him. She
began to tremble, every nerve in her body desperately
aware of him. Slowly he lowered his head, and it
seemed to take for ever until his mouth touched hers.
Fire ran through her blood. He kissed her deeply, his
mouth parting hers with hungry expertise. He released
her chin when he felt her response, pulling the pins
from her hair, running his fingers through the
loosened softness. Then he released her, abruptly, a
muscle flicking in his jaw as he stared down at her.

Lise scrambled out of the car, hardly able to breathe, mumbling goodnight as she shut the door.

Jordon let her go, watching her as she ran up the steps to the front door. She stepped inside without looking back, and heard the roar of the engine as it fired into life.

The telephone in the hall was ringing. Absently she moved towards it and picked up the receiver, her ears still straining to hear the sound of Jordon's car.

The voice on the other end crackled noisily. 'Lise? Lise?'

'Yes?' She listened, unable to imagine who could be telephoning her at this time of night.

'Where the hell have you been? I've been calling for hours!' It was Meredith, petulant and very angry. Lise's attention focused sharply on her cousin's voice, utterly surprised to be speaking to her. They hadn't been in touch since Lise left America.

'I've been out to dinner,' she explained coolly. 'Meredith, where are you ringing from? Are you——?'

'Listen,' Meredith cut in irritably. 'Mason is very ill. He's had a massive heart attack, and he might not pull through.'

Lise paled, her hand tightening on the receiver, knuckles gleaming white. 'When?' she whispered in horror. 'How is he?'

Meredith didn't answer. 'He's been asking for you,' she said, her voice making it clear that she couldn't for a moment understand why. 'You ought to come immediately—he might not have much time left.'

Lise's mind was whirling. She felt sick with worry about her grandfather, and the practical details of arranging an immediate flight to San Francisco defeated her. Meredith had been very brutal, not bothering to cushion the tragic news.

'I haven't the money . . .' she began faintly, still confused.

'I didn't suppose you would have,' interrupted Meredith scathingly, her voice sounding so clear and close she could have been calling from the next street. 'Nancy has arranged everything. There's a ticket waiting for you at Heathrow. You're booked on a flight that leaves London at nine a.m. your time, tomorrow. There will be somebody here to meet you when you arrive.'

'Thank you, and thanks for ringing and telling me,' Lise said with grateful relief.

'I didn't have much choice,' replied Meredith stonily. 'Orders from Nancy.' The receiver clicked and Lise realised that her cousin had hung up. As she slowly replaced the receiver, she caught sight of her reflection in the tiny gilt-framed mirror above the telephone. Her face was deathly white, her eyes haunted and enormous.

'Don't die!' she whispered out loud, willing her thoughts across the ocean to her grandfather. 'Please don't die!'

CHAPTER FOUR

LISE didn't go to bed that night. There was too much to do, and she couldn't have slept anyway. She left the flat early and got a taxi to the airport, arriving in plenty of time.

It was a dark, overcast morning and the taxi driver grumbled half-heartedly about the rain all the way. Lise sat in the back, stiff and cold, unable to say a word. She had tried to phone Meredith back, but there had been no answer, either at the apartment or at Angela's house. She didn't even know what hospital Mason was in. She had been so shaken by Meredith's call that she hadn't had the presence of mind to find out the important details.

As her cousin had promised, a first class ticket was waiting for her at the airline check-in desk. She duly checked in and watched her hastily packed suitcase disappearing along the conveyor belt.

'You'll be boarding in about an hour, Miss Holbrook,' the girl at the desk told her with an efficient smile. Lise nodded and made her way over to the pay telephones.

She tried Angela's house again. No answer. She dialled Mason's apartment next and jumped as the receiver was picked up at the other end. It was Nancy, and she almost died with relief.

'How is he?' she demanded tremulously.

'He's holding his own,' Nancy told her, her voice heavy with that relief that comes after a long period of waiting. 'You know what a tough old bird he is.'

'Thank God!' Lise closed her eyes, leaning weakly against the phone booth. 'Meredith didn't tell me any details, and my imagination has been working overtime.'

'Isn't that typical of her?' Nancy retorted angrily. 'I was going to call you myself, but I was with Mason and I didn't want to leave him, so I asked Meredith to do it for me. Where are you?'

Lise explained, and when she replaced the receiver some moments later she felt a good deal better.

Nancy had been kind and reassuring. Lise knew now that her grandfather would be alive when she got to San Francisco. That had been her constant fear during the night, that he might not make it, that she might never see him again. She bought herself some coffee and wandered back to the pay phones. She had two more calls to make.

Jerri answered sleepily, coming wide awake as Lise briefly explained the situation.

'Oh God, I'm sorry! I hope he pulls through.'

'So do I.' Lise felt her eyes filling with tears. Everything seemed unreal. It was crazy that she should be standing here in the bustle of Heathrow Airport waiting for a flight to San Francisco. Life suddenly seemed very precarious.

'Don't worry about the audition,' said Jerri soothingly. 'I'll sort it out with Joe. And Lise . . . keep in touch!'

'I will. Thanks.' There was a lump in her throat and she could hardly speak.

Her final call was to the house. Shaun picked up the phone almost immediately.

'I was on my way out,' he explained cheerfully. 'Oh, and by the way, you had some calls last night. A woman——'

'I know,' Lise cut in, and had to explain about Mason all over again. 'Will you tell Mrs Collins I don't know how long I'll be away. And will you keep an eye on my flat?'

'Sure.' Shaun sounded deflated, even though he was trying to be sympathetic.

'Shaun, I'm sorry about last night,' she apologised again, feeling that she had to put it right somehow.

'It's okay.' There was a pause, then he said. 'I suppose it's serious between you and Jordon Hayes?'

Lise was silent for a second. 'I don't know,' she said at last.

'Which says it all,' replied Shaun drily. 'I'll see you when I see you.' He put the receiver down rather abruptly, and she knew that he was still hurt. There was nothing she could do to change that; she had never encouraged him. Except last night, a tiny voice in her head reminded her. She couldn't change that either.

When her flight was called, she made her way to the gate, along with a knot of other passengers, and boarded the plane. The first class section had huge, comfortable seats, and all the passengers were issued with blankets, pillows and slippers as they sat down.

Lise slipped off her jacket and settled down by the window. Outside it was raining heavily, the tarmac shining, the airport buildings grey and drab.

Across the aisle sat a well-dressed American woman with a girl who was obviously her daughter. The girl smiled at Lise with nervous eyes as the plane taxied down the runway in preparation for take-off. Lise smiled back. She never felt nervous about flying. Usually she enjoyed it, but this time the flight seemed to last for ever.

Throughout the eleven-and-a-half-hour journey the

stewardesses patrolled the aisles with free drinks and hot meals. Lise drank fruit juice and water, feeling her skin drying up as the hours passed. She felt exhausted but she couldn't sleep. She tried to concentrate on the in-flight films and on the magazines she had bought at the airport, but found it impossible. Her grandfather filled her thoughts. How would he be, how would he greet her after three years' estrangement? She was gripped by apprehension and loneliness, and she had no one to talk to.

Jordon. He came into her mind and her heart ached. She needed his strength now. She checked her thoughts, her eyes clouding. The need shocked her. She had never needed anybody before. She wished she could have got in touch with him before she left, but even if she'd found the courage, she had no idea where he stayed when he was in England. She let her mind drift back over the evening they had spent together. She knew him a little better now, and felt more fascinated, more intrigued by him than ever, though he still had the power to frighten the life out of her.

He was hard and tough. The harshness of his life had moulded him into the sophisticated, intelligent, successful man he was now. She had seen a wild streak in him, a ruthless self-will. He knew exactly what he wanted. He forced the world to give in to him and she guessed that he invariably got what he wanted. But she had also glimpsed another side of him, a warm, charming, gentle side, and it was this combination, together with his potent physical magnetism, that she found overpoweringly attractive.

Oh, but she had made such a fool of herself last night. She had been tongue-tied, and more than likely deadly boring. Jordan would be used to women who sparked with beauty, wit and intelligence. The woman in the gold dress, Diana de la Mesengère, sprang to mind. Lise had forgotten all about her.

What does it matter? she thought defeatedly; she probably wouldn't see Jordon again now that she was leaving London. He might not have got in touch again anyway.

She looked around the darkened cabin, feeling restless. Many people were asleep, stretched out across the seats. The film was still flickering away, a number of passengers listening on headphones. The journey seemed interminable.

The pilot's voice, flat and dehumanised, came over the tannoy system from time to time, advising the passengers of points of interest to be seen out of the windows. Lise stared down at the green and orange patchwork of Ohio, her mind jumbled with thoughts of Mason and Jordon, willing the plane to reach San Francisco.

Then at last it began its slow descent towards the runway of San Francisco International Airport. It was just after noon, local time. Lise collected her suitcase, clearing Customs and Immigration after queueing for thirty minutes. She felt tired and stiff as she made her way towards the noisy Arrivals Lounge.

Nancy was waiting to meet her, and Lise rushed into her arms, her eyes filling with tears.

'Oh, Nancy, I'm *so* glad to see you!' she exclaimed.

Nancy hadn't changed at all. She was a tall, elegant woman in her early fifties; her clothes were expensively chic, her dark hair perfectly coiffured. She had a calm, incisive mind, and her dark eyes were kind as she smiled at Lise. 'I'm glad you came. I knew you would.'

As they drove along the busy Bayshore Freeway towards downtown San Francisco, Lise asked about her grandfather. Out of the windows of Mason's long, chauffeur-driven car, she could see the bay glittering in the sunshine, the tall skyscrapers thrusting up into the clouds, and at any other time she would have been happy to be back. San Francisco was an exciting city, beautiful in a fierce, modern way. Now she looked round with little interest, her thoughts elsewhere.

'He was told to take it easy,' Nancy was saying worriedly. 'He's not as young as he thinks he is. Louis has been warning him for months. A man of his age should be thinking of retirement.'

'What would he do?' Lise smiled tiredly.

'I know, I know,' admitted Nancy. 'But if he carries on the way he has been doing, he'll kill himself.'

Under the stern exterior, Lise could see that Nancy was very upset. She had been with Mason for many years. She had started as his private secretary, and he had been impressed by her quiet efficiency. When his housekeeper left after a blazing row, Nancy just happened to be changing apartments. She took over that job as well, moving into the suite of rooms in Mason's apartment. She was his hostess, his friend, his nursemaid. She was utterly indispensable.

Lise had always favoured the opinion that Nancy was in love with Mason. She acted like a wife, she worried like a wife. Why had Mason never married her? she wondered now. Lise's grandmother had died young, but Mason had never remarried. He was closer to Nancy than anybody else.

Lise wasn't close enough to either of them to ask. Personal questions had never been encouraged by Mason—there was a remote streak running through the whole family. Perhaps too much money encouraged it: greed made people very spiteful and very suspicious. Lise sighed. She couldn't pretend she was looking forward to seeing the rest of the family again.

The car drew to a silent halt and she realised that they were in front of the apartment building where her grandfather lived.

She turned to Nancy, her eyes questioning. 'I thought we'd be going straight to the hospital . . .?'

Nancy smiled reassuringly. 'You need some sleep, my dear. You're dead on your feet.'

'Oh, but——'

'I'll take you to the hospital this evening. Mason sleeps for most of the day, anyway. He's under sedation.'

Lise gave in. She did feel exhausted and she longed for a cool shower.

The tall apartment building was on California Street, right at the top of Nob Hill. It was practically next door to the exclusive Pacific Union Club, of which Mason was a member, and only a stone's throw away from Grace Cathedral. Lise climbed out of the car, her legs unsteady, the sunlight blinding her. The traffic rushed by, the sounds of the city filling her ears. Nancy took her arm and ushered her into the private lift that whisked them up to the penthouse apartment.

Noticing Lise's expression, she asked, 'How does it feel to be back?'

Lise shrugged. 'Strange. Three years is a long time. I feel as though I'm dreaming.'

'Mason always regretted your leaving,' said Nancy quietly.

'Did he? Why didn't he answer my letters, then?' Lise let her lashes sweep down over her eyes. She couldn't help sounding reproachful.

Nancy touched her arm. 'I'm sure he wanted to, but you know what he's like. He's got the pride of the devil; he decides something and that's that—he won't

give in or change course. It's made him a successful
businessman and it's ruined his private life. Whatever
the rights and wrongs of the situation, both Jack and
your mother disappointed him. It hit him hard; he's
still trying to live with it.' She paused, smiling ruefully.
'I'm not trying to excuse him—I know how cruel and
inflexible he can be. I'm just trying to tell you that he
does care. He's been asking for you ever since he had
the coronary.'

'He will be all right?' asked Lise huskily, needing to
hear Nancy say yes again.

Nancy nodded. 'If he takes things easy. It was touch
and go for a while, but he's over the crisis now. You'll
see for yourself this evening. He *is* getting better—but
don't expect too much.'

The lift stopped, the doors sliding open. The
apartment had been redecorated, Lise realised as her
feet sank into the deep-pile, off-white carpet. On one
of the plush white leather sofas sat Meredith, idly
flicking through a copy of *Vogue*. She was as beautiful
and as glamorous as ever, Lise thought, from the top of
her sleek blonde head down to the expensive hand-
made shoes she wore on her feet.

'Hello, Meredith.' Lise walked forward, smiling.
Her cousin looked up, wide blue eyes sliding over Lise
in a bored way.

'Hi.' She didn't return the smile. She didn't stand
up. 'Rough flight?'

And she was as bitchy as ever, Lise realised ruefully.
Compared to Meredith's glossy perfection, she probably did look a mess, she thought, glancing down at
her pale, printed cotton trousers and casual white
jacket.

'Not particularly. Is first class ever rough?' she
parried drily.

Meredith shrugged her elegant shoulders without answering. She was obviously not in a friendly mood. Nothing had changed.

'Would you like some coffee?' Nancy bustled cheerfully, breaking the silence, trying to smooth things over.

Lise shook her head. 'No, thanks, but I'd love a shower and a nap before we go to the hospital.'

'Of course. You know where your room is. I'll have a tray sent up.'

'My room?' She was surprised and it showed.

'Oh, yes. Mason wouldn't allow me to change a thing,' laughed Nancy.

Lise ran up the wide polished stairs and into her old bedroom. Her suitcase had already arrived, lying on a stand at the foot of the bed. Everything was exactly the same. It was a large, square room, huge windows taking up one wall, the others pastel pink, the carpet cream, rose-patterned.

The view from the windows was breathtakingly familiar. The jagged San Francisco skyline, the TransAmerica Pyramid, and beyond, the smooth blue waters of the bay.

A high four-poster bed stood against the wall opposite the windows, covered in a snowy white quilt. All around, her ornaments and books were in their same places. There were even a few favourite toys from her childhood. In the centre of the room were two white sofas arranged around a low wooden table, which held a bowl of sweet-smelling roses.

Lise walked over to the wardrobes and pulled open the doors. All her clothes were there. She stared at them, a strange feeling in her stomach. It was like going back in time, as though she had never been away. Memories flooded back, memories she thought she had forgotten, episodes from her childhood: friends, birthday parties, Christmas parties. A lot of the clothes were hopelessly out of fashion now, but the glittering, expensive evening dresses from New York were timeless. She pulled one out—a simple magnolia crêpe sheath. She had worn it only once. It had fitted her like a second skin, sexy yet demure. She smiled. At eighteen she hadn't liked it much, now she could appreciate just how beautiful it was. It had been hanging in this wardrobe for three years, yet she could wear it tonight at the most expensive restaurant in town. Quality like that lasted.

A wave of tiredness washed over her. She hung back the dress and wandered into the bathroom. Nancy had thoughtfully provided a basket of toiletries for her use, and a huge vase of roses scented the air.

On the glass shelf over the pale pink basin stood crystal flagons of perfume. Lise pulled the stopper from one of them and held it to her nostrils. It was heavenly—a deliciously light scent of flowers by Van Cleef. Smiling at Nancy's kindness, and making a mental note to thank her, Lise stripped off her clothes and stepped into the marble shower. It was wonderful to wash away the tired staleness of a long flight, and as she stepped out and reached for a thick fluffy towel, she reflected again how luxurious the apartment was.

She had accepted this way of life as normal when she lived here. She had been little more than a child then, and perhaps more than a little of the spoiled brat Mason had accused her of being before she left! Three years in London, earning her own living, had changed her. She had grown up, developed her own character. She could appreciate this fantastic place now, without expecting it as her right.

In the bedroom, she rummaged through her suitcase

to find a nightdress. A tray of sandwiches and coffee had been brought in while she was in the shower, but she felt too tired to touch them. Yawning, she climbed into bed, and was asleep before her head touched the pillow.

Nancy woke her at eight with a pot of fresh coffee. She dressed, still feeling exhausted. Jet lag, she supposed, a dart of apprehension shooting through her at the thought of seeing Mason again.

As she brushed her hair in front of the mirror, she thought of Jordon, and realised that she had dreamt about him again. A wistful longing twisted inside her, a longing to see him, a longing to touch him. He was so far away. Angrily she pushed the thoughts from her mind and went to find Nancy.

The hospital was very quiet. Nancy led her straight to Mason's rooms. 'I'll wait out here,' she said as they reached the door.

'Come in with me,' begged Lise, because she knew Nancy wanted to see Mason, and because, if she was honest, she needed a little moral support.

The room was pleasant enough, in a slightly antiseptic way. There were flowers everywhere. Her grandfather was lying in the centre of a huge, metal-framed bed, surrounded by complicated-looking electronic equipment that was emitting high-pitched noises at regular intervals.

His eyes were closed. He looked old, Lise thought, and frail. His skin held a greyish tinge. Her heart turned over.

A young, pretty nurse bustled towards them as they walked in. 'Don't stay too long,' she said, softening the words with a smile.

'How is he today, nurse?' asked Nancy, her eyes on Mason.

'Much better. He gets stronger every day,' the nurse replied cheerfully. Then, lowering her voice, she said, 'He's talking about discharging himself. Try to talk him out of it, will you?'

Nancy frowned. 'I'll try,' she promised.

'Me too,' added Lise, though she doubted that anyone could stop her grandfather doing what he wanted.

At the sound of her voice, Mason's eyes flickered open. 'Lise? Is that you?'

'Yes, Grandpa, it's me.' She hurried over to the bed, a lump in her throat as she took his cold hand in her own. 'How do you feel?'

'Better. Much better for seeing you.' He patted her hand, and she was surprised by his strength. The greyness had disappeared from his face, and his eyes were hard and clear. I must have been mistaken, she thought. He doesn't look old or frail; he looks as indomitable as ever.

'Good.' She smiled sweetly at him, realising how foolish they had both been. Pride had separated them for three years. When somebody came close to death, you realised how unimportant the trivial day-to-day fights were. You realised how they veiled the things that mattered.

Nancy had been hovering by the door, and Mason called her over to the bedside.

'I'm discharging myself tomorrow,' he told her bluntly. 'Can you arrange it for me?'

'No,' replied Nancy, just as bluntly. 'You know what Louis said—you need rest.'

'I can get all the rest I need at home,' Mason cut in irritably. 'I'm dying of boredom lying here in this room. Dammit, there's nothing else they can do for me here!'

Lise squeezed his hand gently. 'You ought to do what Louis says.'

Mason rolled his eyes. 'Women!' He said it as though he was swearing. 'If you don't sort it out for me, Nancy, you'll be looking for another job.'

Nancy shrugged. 'So, fire me,' she said flatly. 'If you want to kill yourself, that's fine. Just don't expect me to help you.'

Two days later, Mason left hospital, despite rigorous protests from Louis Salvador, his doctor, and from Nancy and Lise. But there was nothing anybody could do to stop him. He had made up his mind and that was that. So Nancy employed a full-time nurse to live in at the apartment. Nurse Freedman was highly qualified. She was a tall, thin, very stern lady in her mid-fifties, with wiry grey hair and a lined face. And it soon became clear that she wasn't in the least afraid of Mason's terrible temper. She treated him like a recalcitrant child: she made him stay in bed and she made him eat the food that Louis suggested, and take his medicine. And every time she caught him on the telephone, making business calls that had been strictly forbidden by Louis, she pounced, her strident voice ringing through the apartment.

Lise spent a lot of time with him in his mahogany-furnished bedroom. They played chess most afternoons. Mason always won. If it looked, at any time, as if Lise might be winning, he would cheat unashamedly to reverse the position. He seemed to be making a remarkable recovery, and appeared stronger every day.

Their time spent together drew them closer. Neither mentioned the row that had precipitated Lise's move to England, but Mason seemed genuinely interested in her acting career.

A week passed pleasantly. Lise began to feel at
home, falling into a daily routine.

One evening, when she got back hot and tired from
an afternoon shopping with Nancy on Union Square,
she heard voices in the lounge, one of them belonging
to Meredith.

She had hardly seen her cousin since her arrival
back. She deposited her shopping and walked into the
room, smiling.

Meredith was pouring drinks and a man was
lounging indolently against the bar. He was tall, wide-
shouldered and dark.

He turned as Lise said cheerfully, 'Union Square
has certainly——'

She stopped, mid-sentence, as her eyes met those of
Jordon Hayes.

CHAPTER FIVE

'HELLO, Lise.' Jordon was smiling at her open-mouthed surprise, but his grey eyes were serious as they slid over her. He was the very last person she had expected to see, and she found herself lost for words.

She stared at him, her heart beating very fast. He dominated the room, fiercely masculine in a black dinner-jacket and dark trousers. Her glance lingered on his face, the darkness of his eyes, the strong, mobile mouth, the glinting blackness of his hair.

'You two know each other?' Meredith asked, obviously surprised.

'We . . . I . . .' began Lise, floundering, and Jordon cut in smoothly.

'We met in London.'

Meredith's perfect eyebrows rose. 'What a coincidence,' she said very drily, voice questioning.

Jordon smiled, ignoring the unspoken question, his eyes still on Lise. She tried to pull herself together, feeling very foolish.

'How are you?' she managed politely, all the time thinking, what on earth are you doing here? I've been dreaming of you every night, then I come home and you're here.

'Very well,' he replied urbanely, his eyes teasing her. 'You?'

She shrugged, her cheeks flushed with delicate colour. 'Fine.'

Meredith, feeling excluded, not sure what was going on between Lise and Jordon, cut in: 'You're going to be late for dinner, Lise, if you don't hurry and change.'

Her voice was hostile, almost sulky, but it brought Lise to her senses and reminded her that tonight was a special occasion. Mason was being allowed up for dinner for the first time. Nurse Freedman wasn't in favour; she had made her views very clear to Mason during one of their frequent rows, but he had shouted her down, a sure sign that he was almost back to normal.

She felt Jordon's gaze upon her, and her eyes met his for a second.

'Excuse me. As Meredith says, I'll have to go and change,' she said, ridiculously polite and distant, then fled the room without casting him another glance.

In her bedroom, she leant her back against the closed door, and found herself trembling. What was he *doing* here? she wondered for the millionth time. How could he be downstairs with Meredith, cool and charming, acting as though there was absolutely nothing unusual about his presence here at the apartment? Was he staying for dinner? Had he followed her to San Francisco? The idea made her heart sing.

Catching sight of the time, she hurried into the bathroom and turned on the shower. She had to hurry.

As she dried her hair, she chose her dress. It was simple dark green crêpe, with a round neckline and wide sleeves, caught into buttoned cuffs at the wrists. The cut was expensive. It fell flatteringly over the curves of her body, emphasising each graceful movement she made. With it, she wore sheer stockings and green satin high-heeled shoes. The effect was pleasing, the final touch a small emerald brooch at her shoulder that brought out the green of her eyes.

She wanted to look her best, so she spent a lot of time on her make-up, stroking colour on to her eyes and lips, and shaping her heart-shaped face with a touch of pink blusher. Trying to decide whether or not to leave her hair loose, she almost jumped out of her skin at the knock on the door, visibly relaxing as Meredith sauntered into the room.

'I'm nearly ready,' she smiled, imagining that her cousin had come to hurry her along.

'There's plenty of time,' replied Meredith coolly, eyeing Lise's dress. 'Mason is still dressing. I heard him arguing with that old harridan of a nurse as I came past.'

'She's only doing her job,' said Lise mildly. 'I like her.'

'You would.' Meredith smiled contemptuously.

Ignoring that, Lise pulled a comb through her hair, deciding to leave it loose to fall around her shoulders.

'I love your dress,' she said truthfully. Meredith looked stunning. Like Lise, she was tall and blonde, though totally different in looks. Meredith had wide blue eyes and smooth, tanned skin. Her dress was cream silk jersey, with a floating cream silk jacket; her jewellery was heavy, burnished gold. She looked rich and sexy. She's a million times more beautiful than me, Lise thought ruefully, totally unaware of her own sensual innocence.

'Thanks,' Meredith replied, accepting the compliment as though it was her right. She perched herself delicately on the edge of the sofa, and silence fell between the two girls.

'How long have you known Jordon Hayes?' asked Meredith suddenly.

Lise turned to look at her in surprise. 'Not long—a couple of weeks.'

'How did you meet?' Meredith's eyes were cold as she fired the question.

'He saw a play I was in. There was a party afterwards at a club and I met him there,' explained Lise, frowning slightly at something in her cousin's face. 'I couldn't believe it when I walked in just now and there he was.'

Meredith smiled, eyes cruel. 'Why not? I invited him to dinner.'

Confused, Lise said, 'You know him?' She had convinced herself that he had come to see her, but as she spoke, she answered the question for herself. She suddenly remembered how surprised Meredith had been to find that Lise and Jordon knew each other, which meant . . .

'Of course,' the older girl laughed. 'He's very well known in this city.'

'I know.'

Meredith's smile faded, her voice becoming hard. 'And this is a friendly warning, dear cousin. Stay away from him. He's private property.'

Lise couldn't imagine for a second Jordon being anyone's property, but as Meredith's words sank in, she felt as though an ice-cold hand was squeezing her heart. What a fool I've been, she thought miserably. What a stupid, *stupid* fool.

'You mean . . . you mean that you're . . .?' She couldn't finish the sentence.

'Lovers?' Meredith finished it for her. 'More than that, darling. I expect to become Mrs Jordon Hayes in the very near future.'

Lise stared, shocked to the core, hardly able to believe it. A terrible pain clawed inside her.

'It's not official yet,' Meredith continued, carefully watching Lise's face. 'So keep it to yourself. I don't want it leaking out until I'm good and ready.'

Lise nodded, wordlessly, her green eyes dark with a nameless anguish.

Meredith's mouth twisted. 'Aren't you going to congratulate me? You don't seem very pleased.' Her expression changed suddenly, her voice becoming acid. 'My God, don't tell me you had designs on him yourself!'

'No!' Lise answered too quickly, her face scarlet. 'No, of course not.' She had to lie, to try to save some tiny part of her pride from Meredith's contempt.

'I'm glad to hear it.' Her cousin stood up, smoothing down her soft cream dress in one graceful movement. 'Although I suppose I couldn't blame you if you had. Men like Jordon are hardly ten a penny. Most women know that as soon as they see him.' Even you, her eyes said wordlessly.

Lise turned away, fiddling with the catch of the brooch on her dress. 'I wouldn't know,' she said blankly.

Meredith laughed, pressing her advantage home. 'Oh, come now, I saw the way you were looking at him downstairs.'

'I hardly know him,' Lise protested with difficulty. 'We only met a couple of times, and as far as I'm concerned, you're welcome to him, Meredith. I hope you'll both be very happy.' And God forgive the lie, she added silently.

Meredith walked to the door, her expression complacent. 'We will be. See you later.'

Lise stared at her reflection in the mirror as the door closed quietly. Meredith's words were a totally unexpected bombshell, and she didn't know why the thought of Jordon and her cousin marrying was so unendurable to her. There were other questions chasing around in her mind as well. Jordon must have known who she was when they met. He'd said nothing. He had pursued her, kissed her——She closed her eyes, remembering the touch of his mouth, the caress of his hands on her skin. Her body betrayed her, an unsatisfied ache shivering inside her.

He must have been involved with Meredith even then, damn him. Lise groaned, standing up, and walking towards the door. She had never felt less hungry in her life, and the thought of facing Jordon over dinner filled her with apprehension. But because she couldn't let Mason down she made her way downstairs, taking a deep breath as she entered the lounge.

There were other guests as well as the family. As she walked in, her eyes unerringly found Jordon. He was lounging on one of the long leather sofas, talking to a distinguished-looking man in a white dinner-jacket. He looked up, his grey eyes meeting hers, and her heart turned over. He had been waiting for her, she knew, and she looked away, unbearably confused by her response to him after all she had learned.

'Lise, you're late.' Mason arrived at her side, taking her arm. 'Let me fix you a drink, then I'll introduce you to everyone.'

He was in a very good mood, jovial, charming, and he looked well. Lise smiled at him and told him so.

'It's getting away from that damned woman for a few hours,' he snorted cheerfully. Lise couldn't help laughing.

'Poor Nurse Freedman!'

'I told Nancy to fire her,' said Mason baldly. 'I must have fired her myself a hundred times! She won't go!'

'You shouldn't be so mean to her,' Lise reproved gently. 'She's only doing her job.'

'Ha!' Mason was clearly not convinced, and it was
so good to see him up and about again that Lise didn't
say any more.

With a long glass of gin and tonic in her hand, she
allowed her grandfather to steer her around the room,
introducing her to the other guests. Nancy was there,
and Meredith, and Louis Salvador, Mason's doctor
and friend, but there was no sign of Angela or her
husband.

Lise shook hands and smiled, but she hardly heard a
word, hardly noticed the people in front of her. Her
awareness of Jordon, only a few feet away, was
controlling her. She knew that he was watching her,
and it cost her a great effort of will to keep her eyes
averted. But he couldn't be avoided for ever, and she
found herself trembling as Mason inexorably guided
her towards him.

Both men rose as they approached. The man in the
white dinner-jacket was Adam Lawson, a well-known
biographer. Lise recognised the name immediately;
she had read his latest book just before she left
London. It was a point of contact—he was obviously
pleased that she knew his work. He smiled charmingly
and complimented her dress, murmuring something
about beauty and brains. Lise smiled back, her jaw
aching with tension.

'And this, my dear, is Jordon Hayes,' Mason said
cheerfully enough, though Lise saw the wary respect in
his eyes and was surprised by it. 'Jordon is putting in a
takeover bid for Holbrook International. He's got me
running round in circles.'

'We've already been introduced,' Lise said quietly,
not meeting Jordon's eyes, digesting the news about
the takeover. Today she had been hit with one shock
after another, and her mind was reeling.

Mason's brows rose, but he didn't comment.

Adam Lawson started talking, asking about Mason's health, and with a mumbled, 'Excuse me, I must have a word with Nancy,' Lise took the opportunity to escape through the high open windows on to the long balcony. She couldn't have stayed in there for a moment longer; she felt as though she was involved in some sort of ridiculous charade.

She let the balmy night air drift over her and looked out over the city. The skyscrapers were glittering with lights and below she could hear the roar of the traffic, the bells on the cable cars as they made their slow ascent of Nob Hill. She leant against the wrought iron railing, grateful for the peace and solitude, wishing with all her heart that she hadn't got up this morning.

'Why are you out here alone?' Jordon's low voice behind her made her jump. He had followed her. Perhaps, somewhere in her mind, she had known that he would.

She whirled round to face him. He towered over her, wide-shouldered and powerful, his face shadowed in the darkness.

'I needed some air,' she replied breathlessly.

His mouth twisted into a smile. 'You only arrived ten minutes ago.'

'It's hot in there.' She shrugged inadequately.

Jordon shot her a long, hard glance, reaching into his pocket for his cigarette case. He held it out to her, and she shook her head, watching as he placed a cigarette between his lips, watching his face illuminated by soft flame.

'You've been avoiding me,' he remarked.

'Have I?' She lowered her eyes, unable to make a joke of it, or parry wittily.

'Why?' he asked, ignoring her prevarication.

'Why should I?' She looked away, determined not to let him bully her.

Jordon expelled smoke from his mouth impatiently. 'You tell me! I thought we were past all this.'

'Well, you were wrong, then.' Lise's voice sounded stony. In her mind she could picture him holding Meredith, kissing her. She tried to dislodge the image but it wouldn't disappear. It hurt.

Jordon's hands touched her shoulders. 'I don't think so,' he said softly.

Lise's head jerked up. 'Jordon——' she whispered anxiously, but it was too late.

She stood helplessly, watching his mouth come closer, mesmerised by the strong, masculine line of it. By the time it touched hers, she was dizzy, her head spinning, lips parting to return a kiss that held anger mingled with desire.

Her hands moved, grasping his wide, muscled shoulders for support. She heard the swift intake of his breath. He drew her into his arms as their mouths fused hungrily.

It was what she had wanted ever since she walked in today and found him with Meredith. It was what she had been dreaming of, night after night. She was shaking with desire, her bones melting beneath the warm expertise of his mouth.

The kiss went on for ever; Lise's eyes were closed, her body held tightly against the hard strength of his. The noise of somebody approaching broke them apart. There was a mumbled apology, embarrassed laughter and a hasty retreat.

Reluctantly, Jordon let her go, staring down at her, his breath coming quickly, his eyes very dark. She lowered her eyes, wondering who had interrupted them, which brought Meredith back into her mind with a painful rush.

'We ought to get back to the party,' she said tautly.

Jordon nodded, aware of her sudden withdrawal.
'Lise——'

'Mason will be wondering where I am,' she cut in
quickly, before he could speak.

'Running away again?' he queried, smiling.

'Yes.' She flashed him a look from beneath her
lashes. She turned, walked away, then stopped. She
wanted to ask him about Meredith, found she couldn't
and instead asked, 'Are you really trying to take over
Holbrook International?'

'Yes.'

Lise glimpsed his ruthlessness and backed away
from it. 'Mason will fight you,' she said fiercely. 'The
company has been his whole life.'

Jordon shook his head. 'He won't. I hold the
winning hand.'

Not understanding, Lise walked away from him,
back into the noisy warmth of the lounge.

Dinner seemed to last for hours. The dining-room,
though formal, held an air of intimacy. The rectangu-
lar table was mahogany, as were the carved dining
chairs. Over the table hung a huge chandelier that lent
a warm glow to the silver and crystal and china with
which the table was laid. The walls of the room were a
pinky-brown colour, lined with part of Mason's
collection of equine portraits. The colour gave the
room warmth, despite its size.

Seated next to her grandfather and opposite Jordon,
Lise kept her head down, trying to concentrate on the
delicious food in front of her. She let the conversation
flow over her, though when addressed directly, she
answered, smiling. She was aware of every word
Jordon said, deeply aware of every movement he

made, every indolent gesture. He was witty and clever and very charming. And she noticed that her grandfather was also listening—unusual for him. It made her realise just how important Jordon was. He commanded Mason's respect, and not many did.

I think I'm falling in love with him. The thought flashed into her mind unbidden, stopping her in her tracks.

Meredith is going to marry him, she told herself desperately, but that only brought pain, and didn't change anything.

She looked up and found him staring at her, his expression unreadable but intent. She looked away and caught Meredith's hard, sullen glance from the other end of the table. How can I care for him like this? she wondered despairingly, not even knowing when it had begun. Had it already been too late when their eyes met for the first time? She suspected so. He had never been out of her mind from that very first moment.

When she tried to think about it logically, she knew it was impossible, insane. He was going to marry Meredith. He was going to take over Mason's empire. The thoughts disturbed her more than she cared to admit.

When the meal was over, family and guests drifted back into the lounge. Mason was looking tired. The physical effort of the dinner party had drained him, and his face was drawn, his eyes glazed. Nancy ushered him off to bed with the aid of Nurse Freedman, and Lise took the opportunity to escape too. Her last glimpse of Jordon was taken surreptitiously. Meredith was standing close to him, her red-tipped fingers on his arm in an openly intimate caress, and he was smiling down at her indulgently. Sickened,

Lise retreated to the sanctuary of her bedroom, although she knew she wouldn't sleep.

The following day, she was up very early. She disguised the tell-tale shadows of a restless night with make-up, before making her way to her grandfather's room.

Nurse Freedman admitted her with a cheerful smile. 'He's not so clever today,' she said in a low, confidential voice. 'He overdid it last night.'

'What the hell are you two mumbling about over there?' Mason demanded testily from his bed.

Nurse Freedman pulled a face at Lise, her expression revealing just what she had to put up with from her patient.

'Would you like me to bring you some coffee?' she asked, noting Lise's tired eyes. 'I was just going to make some for myself.'

Lise nodded gratefully, and moved to sit by her grandfather's bed.

'How are you today, Grandpa?' she asked gently.

'Fine,' replied Mason brusquely. 'As usual, that woman is fussing unnecessarily.'

Knowing that it was useless to argue, even though he looked pale and exhausted, she said brightly, 'It was a lovely dinner party last night.'

Mason eyed her shrewdly. 'You didn't seem to be enjoying yourself.'

'I had a headache, I'm afraid,' replied Lise untruthfully, unable to explain the real reason for her unsociable behaviour.

He snorted, not taken in for a second. 'What do you think of Jordon Hayes?' he demanded suddenly.

Surprised by the question, Lise couldn't help the betraying flush of colour that stained her cheeks at the mention of his name.

'I hardly know the man,' she said hurriedly.

Mason watched her reaction carefully, not missing one of the fleeting emotions showing on her face.

'He's tough.' He spoke evenly, as though he was warning her.

'Yes.' Lise stood up, walking over to the windows. The bay was shrouded in mist, the skyscrapers cut off by low cloud. Later it would clear and the sun would come out.

'What did you mean last night, when you said that Jordon Hayes is trying to take over the company?' she asked, without turning round.

'Nothing for you to worry about, baby. Just business.'

She listened to his voice, trying to gauge whether or not he was telling the truth. A feeling of foreboding was settling over her like a black cloud. There was something wrong. She didn't know how she knew, but she did.

'Grandpa——' She turned, wanting to tell him how sure Jordon had been, but his eyes were closed. He was asleep.

She crept out of the room, very quietly. Nurse Freedman was just arriving with a tray of coffee.

'I'll just check on him,' she said, when Lise explained the situation.

Lise waited for her to reappear. 'Is he okay?'

'Sure.' The nurse was as cheerful as ever. 'He wore himself out last night, that's all. It was a bit too much for him. You know what he's like though, nobody can make him stay in that bed!'

That was the problem. Mason was so irascible, so used to getting his own way. His over-exertion didn't help his recovery. It was a problem that preyed on Lise's mind as she took a taxi to the Cannery, where she had arranged to meet Nancy for lunch.

Situated near Fisherman's Wharf, it was a magnificent three-storey, red brick building, once the site of
the Del Monte company's canning plant. Now
revitalised, it had been turned into a complex of shops,
art galleries and restaurants. There was a central
courtyard, full of trees and plants, a popular gathering
place for tourists and residents alike, especially at
lunchtime.

A crowd had gathered to watch a free magic show,
performed by two young men in dark suits. Lise
walked through, smiling as she heard the children
laughing, and made her way up to the top floor, where
she found Nancy already waiting for her in the chic
glass and chrome salad bar where they had arranged
to meet. It was crowded with lunchtime trade but the
waiter found them a window table. The view was
magnificent. Out in the blue waters of the bay lay
Alcatraz, the grim island prison from which no one
had ever escaped. And to their left, spanning the
distance between San Francisco and Marin County,
was the rusty orange Golden Gate Bridge.

Nancy had spent the morning at Mason's office. By
her side there was a leather briefcase crammed with
papers.

'You look worried,' remarked Lise, as she scanned
the menu.

Nancy didn't answer, and the waiter appeared at
that moment to take their orders. They both ordered
quiche and green salad, and decided on a bottle of dry
white wine.

When the food was in front of them, Lise asked
again, 'Is something wrong?' She could see that Nancy
was preoccupied; she was pushing her salad around
her plate, not touching a thing.

She looked up apologetically as Lise spoke. 'Sorry,
I'm lousy company today.'

'Is it Mason?'

Nancy shrugged, putting down her knife and fork.
'Partly. I'm at my wits' end, trying to keep him in bed.
He's retarding his recovery.'

'Oh, Nancy,' sighed Lise. 'You're not responsible.
There's nothing any of us can do. Mason makes his
own choices.' She tried to reassure the older woman,
even though she felt worried too.

'I spoke to Louis this morning. He said the same
thing.'

'He's the doctor. Listen to him,' Lise urged. Then,
'There's something else, isn't there?' she probed
intuitively.

Nancy looked at her, as though deciding whether or
not to confide. 'You'll have to know sooner or later, I
suppose.' She sipped her wine, replacing the glass on
the table before continuing. 'Holbrook International
is in trouble.'

'What do you mean, trouble?' Lise felt her stomach
turning over. Jordon's words came into her mind: 'I
hold the winning hand.'

Nancy's eyes were troubled. 'To start at the
beginning—some months ago, Mason was offered a
fantastic opportunity to invest in new oil fields being
drilled in South East Asia. He fought off a lot of tough
competition to secure the deal; the expected returns
were phenomenal.' Her shoulders lifted resignedly. 'It
was a risk, because he had to sink a lot of his capital
into plant, and into research and development, but
you know Mason, he loves taking risks. He's built up
the company on risks.'

Lise nodded. A great deal of her grandfather's
reputation was based on the fact that he had a good

nose for a deal. He took chances, and until now had always come through.

'He got backing from a number of major banks,' continued Nancy. 'The assets of Holbrook International were his collateral. I don't know, the reports were all favourable, there was oil out there and Mason looked set to make the killing of his career.'

'What happened?' asked Lise dully.

'The government became unstable. The oil was going to put the country on the map, and the power struggles started. Out of the blue, the government was overthrown in a military coup. The new régime aren't honouring any agreements. The deal is off, and Mason can't recover his investments.' Nancy's eyes filled with tears. 'The stress he's been under these past months brought on his heart attack, I'm sure of it.'

Lise frowned. 'What about the company?'

'That's why I've been into the office this morning. The shares are plummeting, and the banks are pressing us to go into liquidation.' Nancy took out a handkerchief, dabbing her eyes. 'Mason could lose everything. I feel so helpless, Lise; there's nothing I can do. The only person who can help is Jordon Hayes.'

Lise drew breath sharply. 'Jordon Hayes?' she echoed weakly.

Nancy smiled. 'He's a very rich man. His reputation is good. He can restore confidence in the company if his name is linked with it.'

'And what will happen to Grandpa?'

'I don't know.' Nancy shook her head. 'For his health's sake, he should retire, though I don't suppose he will. If Jordon Hayes invests, he will have the controlling interest. Mason will have to step down as head of the company.'

Lise frowned. 'Why should Jordon Hayes step in and save a company that's in so much trouble?'

'He has the money to put it back on its feet. Holbrook International will consolidate his interests across the country. It will put Mr Hayes in an extremely powerful position.'

It was worse than Lise had imagined. Her grandfather's ill health was worrying enough, but to find that he was on the verge of losing his business empire came as a terrible shock. The company was his life. It meant everything to him.

Jordon's involvement didn't surprise her. The dinner party had prepared her. It somehow seemed inevitable, though she couldn't help wondering what perverse fate had involved him so deeply in her life, in all their lives. If he stepped in and saved Holbrook International, it would be because it was a viable business proposition. He was a ruthless man. She didn't imagine he would show any sentiment in business. Given the same situation in reverse though, she knew that her grandfather would do the same. It was the everyday, dog-eat-dog world of big business, and she hated it.

Nancy left early to get back to the office and Lise made her way out of the Cannery, intending to get a taxi back to the apartment.

Standing on the pavement, hoping to hail a passing cab, she was so deep in thought she didn't notice the long black chauffeur-driven car pulling up in front of her. Two people stepped out, and she recognised with a pang of shock Jordon and Diana de la Mesengère.

Jordon smiled. 'Hello, Lise.'

Lise ignored him, her eyes on the woman who was holding his arm. She was wearing a white linen suit that perfectly offset her dark beauty, and she was smiling too.

'We meet again,' she said to Lise, her voice friendly.

Lise automatically returned the smile, nodding, not sure what to say.

Diana turned to Jordon, reaching up to kiss his cheek. 'Lunch was lovely, darling, thank you. I'll see you tomorrow. Don't forget. Eight thirty—and don't be late!' She looked at Lise. 'Nice to see you again.' Then she was gone, disappearing through the arched gateways of the Cannery.

'You look lost.' There was a teasing note in Jordon's voice, and Lise flushed.

'I'm on my way home. I had lunch with Nancy,' she added, not knowing why she was telling him.

Jordon opened the door of the black car. 'Get in. I'll give you a lift.'

'No——' she recoiled, stepping backwards, still hurting from seeing him with Diana de la Mesengère.

'Get in,' he repeated, and the command in his voice had her moving without thought.

The interior of the car was extremely luxurious, rich with the scent of leather and tobacco. Lise huddled against the far window, not looking at the man beside her. She had already taken in every detail of his appearance in the first split second of their meeting. His business suit was dark blue, beautifully cut to his lean, powerful body. His shirt was a very pale blue, his tie darker.

His nearness made her tremble inside. She felt close to tears with the pain of seeing him smile at another woman, kissing another woman. The silence lengthened. She knew he was watching her and felt unnerved.

'Does Meredith know?' She heard her own voice. It was sharp and accusing.

'Does Meredith know what?' he countered coolly.

Lise turned to him angrily, green eyes flashing. 'That you have other lovers?'

Her mouth shook as she realised that this had nothing to do with Meredith. She was asking for herself.

Jordan laughed. 'Why should that concern Meredith?'

'Because——' She stopped abruptly. He was playing games with her. 'I thought . . . well, I thought that you and Meredith . . .'

Cool grey eyes held hers, devastating her. 'I have no interest in Meredith,' he told her without emphasis, and reaching out, ran one long finger gently down her cheek. 'It's you that I want, Lise but then you know that.'

Her heart was pounding. His cool admission of desire made her mouth as dry as sand. She thought about Diana de la Mesengère, about Meredith, and couldn't believe his heartlessness.

'I don't know,' she whispered, her skin on fire where he had touched her. 'And I don't understand . . .'

There was some strange spell binding them together inside the expensive confines of the car. Lise looked into his darkening eyes and felt as though she was drowning. She wanted to cling to him to save herself.

'No?' His smile was gentle. 'I want you,' he repeated softly. 'And you ought to know that I always get what I want.'

'Like Holbrook International?' she whispered.

He nodded. 'Like Holbrook International.'

The car slowed. They were outside the apartment building. Lise couldn't breathe properly. There was a fire inside her, threatening to consume her. Jordon was so calm and certain, every word he said enforced by the hard lines of his face.

'Never!' she said painfully. 'Do you hear me? *Never!*' She had never felt more scared in her life.

CHAPTER SIX

IT was late in the morning. Lise had eaten breakfast alone; she had risen late after another troubled night. Mason was still asleep and Nancy had left early for the office. Lise assumed that Meredith was still in bed.

The older girl had been staying at the apartment for the past week while Angela and her husband were away on business in Toronto. Meredith said she hated being in the house on her own, it frightened her to death, especially as the television news was daily reporting a spate of violent burglaries in the Presidio Heights district.

Lise poured herself more coffee from the silver coffee pot and sipped it slowly, gazing out over the city to a bay still shrouded in mist. Everywhere looked grey, which suited Lise's mood perfectly.

She couldn't stop thinking about Jordon, however hard she tried. A week had passed since he'd given her a lift back from the Cannery, and she had been avoiding him very deliberately since then. He had telephoned twice. The first time she had been out visiting an old school friend in Palo Alto, the second time she had taken the call, and, in her panic, slammed down the receiver as soon as he spoke. It was childish, and it probably only amused him, but she couldn't help herself.

If she saw him, she would become more and more involved with him. He was already woven deep in her heart, inextricably linked with all her thoughts and all her emotions. She was in love with him, but the knowledge brought despair. She had no intention of becoming just another woman in his life, another woman who was crazy about him.

She replaced her cup on its saucer, frowning. She had this conversation with herself every day. She told herself that Jordon was going to marry Meredith, but it didn't make a blind bit of difference; she still couldn't get him out of her mind.

There was a noise behind her and she turned her head, her silver hair swinging around her throat, expecting Meredith, and finding Jordon.

A faint flush crept over her face as their eyes met. She felt sure he knew she had been thinking of him. It was as though her thoughts had brought him to her.

'How did you get in?' she asked sharply. She wondered how long he had been standing, watching her.

'One of the staff let me in,' he said calmly, though his eyes were hard and angry, warning her to mind her tongue.

He walked towards the table, lean and powerful in well-washed jeans and a blue shirt open at the neck, and sat down opposite her. Lise lowered her eyes, allowing her hair to fall around her betraying face. Her heart was beating so hard, she felt sure he would hear it.

He was obviously here to see Meredith, and her heart clenched with ridiculous disappointment as she realised it.

'Would you like some coffee?' she asked, adding quickly, 'Meredith isn't up yet. I could go and——'

'Thank you, I'd like some coffee,' Jordon cut in, and as she looked up at him questioningly, he smiled and said, 'Spend the day with me.'

She frowned, firmly damping down the strange

yearning to do just as he suggested. 'Why?' she demanded baldly.

Jordon moved his head slightly, and a shaft of sunlight struck the darkness of his hair, emphasising the masculine beauty of his features.

'Because I wish it, and because I've booked a table for lunch,' he returned coolly.

'And Meredith?'

His glance hardened. 'To hell with Meredith.'

'I have other plans,' Lise stammered, confused.

Jordon smiled. 'Change them,' he suggested expressionlessly. 'There's somebody I want you to meet.'

That smile turned her legs to water. Trying to pull herself together, she said, 'If you've already booked a table, you must have been pretty sure of me.'

'I decided that you'd been running for far too long,' he said softly.

'Well, I'm sorry to disappoint you . . .'

His eyes held hers. 'You won't be disappointing me,' he drawled lazily, 'because if necessary, I'll put you in the car myself.'

He was immovable, and that unnerved her. Her teeth sank into the softness of her lower lip. 'Don't be silly,' she said nervously, knowing he meant every word. 'I told you, I already have plans for today. Can it be that you're turned down so rarely, you don't know a refusal when you get one?'

The grey eyes gleamed with amusement. 'You have fifteen minutes to get ready,' he said.

'I . . .' Floundering for something to say, some weapon to use against his resolute will, she was interrupted by the arrival of her grandfather, holding Meredith's arm as he walked heavily into the room. 'I won't stay in that damned bed a moment longer!' he was saying angrily, quelling Meredith's protests that he should be resting. 'I'm not a damned invalid!'

Then he saw Lise and Jordon, and smiled, his expression growing speculative. 'Good morning, Lise, Jordon. This is an unexpected surprise.'

Meredith was smiling too. 'A lovely surprise,' she echoed, her eyes on Jordon, warm and promising. She looked stunning, perfectly made up, perfectly coiffured and wearing a scarlet silk dress with matching shoes.

Jordon inclined his dark head to them both, a hard smile touching the corners of his mouth. 'I'm trying to persuade your granddaughter to spend the day with me,' he explained wryly.

Lise's eyes flew to Meredith. Her cousin's mouth hardened into a straight line and her eyes promised Lise trouble to come.

Lise flushed, knowing how it must seem. Meredith looked ready to commit murder.

'I've already explained,' Lise said quickly, 'that I can't possibly——'

'Splendid idea!' Mason cut in, before she could finish. 'Splendid! Lise has been spending far too much time in the apartment. It'll do her the world of good to get out and about in the fresh air. She needs some colour in her cheeks, don't you agree, Meredith?'

He turned to the girl at his side with seemingly complete insensitivity, and Lise cringed inside.

'I'm sure Lise is capable of making up her own mind, Grandfather,' Meredith said very coldly.

Lise winced. 'You promised to have lunch with me today,' she said, turning to Mason, hating this conflict. 'We're in the middle of a game, don't you remember?'

But her grandfather seemed pleased with the situation. 'It'll keep,' he assured her, grinning broadly. 'We can lunch together tomorrow. Now, go and change. You can't keep Jordon waiting all morning.'

It was a *fait accompli*, and Lise was trapped. She looked at Jordon. He had been watching the exchange with amusement, and now his eyes mocked her, daring her to refuse and cause a scene.

Pride stiffened her, rescuing her. 'I'll go and change.' She repeated what Mason had said with contemptuous coolness. 'Fifteen minutes, you said?'

Jordon nodded, watching her as she stood up and walked gracefully from the room.

In her bedroom, she dressed quickly and uncaringly, boiling with anger that she had let herself be outmanoeuvred. She could kill Mason! Pandering to Jordon, just because he was going to save the company!

And she could kill Jordon! He thought he was so clever! He could handle Mason so easily, wielding his power ruthlessly to get what he wanted.

Fuming, Lise glanced at her reflection in the mirror. She'd make him sorry for this! The pale pink skirt with matching short-sleeved blouse and loose bolero looked cool and casual. She clipped back her hair with two tortoiseshell combs and slid her feet into cream leather sandals, then left her room with five minutes of her allotted time left. She had no intention of letting Jordon think she was spending a lot of time getting ready for him.

She met Meredith at the bottom of the stairs. The older girl was still angry and her eyes slid over Lise contemptuously.

'Very innocent,' she remarked acidly, as she took in the pastel pink and Lise's smooth, bare complexion.

'Meredith, I'm sorry——' began Lise, wanting to explain, hating this bitterness between them.

'Sorry?' Meredith cut in savagely. 'Don't make me

laugh! You've been after him ever since you set eyes
on him, you little bitch! I've seen the way you look at
him, everybody has. Do you think it isn't common
knowledge, your schoolgirl crush?'

'What?' Flayed by Meredith's cruelty, Lise paled.

'Oh, I know it amuses Jordon, your adolescent
behaviour. He told me so himself. He has to contend
with that sort of thing all the time,' Meredith sneered,
every word laced with deliberate poison. 'It flatters his
ego, I suppose, to have you——'

'Stop it!' said Lise desperately, imagining Meredith
and Jordon talking about her, laughing about her. 'It
isn't my fault, Meredith, honestly it isn't! Do you
think I want——?'

'I don't care what you want, but believe me, I'm not
just going to stand by and watch you walk away with
Jordon Hayes. God knows he's only doing this to
punish me.' Meredith took a step forwards and Lise
shrank from the hatred in her blue eyes. 'I know what
you're doing, I knew the moment you arrived, so
concerned about Mason's health. But surprise, surprise, Mason's going to lose everything, so you're
transferring your . . . affections,' the word was spoken
scathingly, 'to a more profitable source.'

Unable to stand any more, Lise turned and walked
away in silence, aware of Meredith's eyes boring
malevolently into her back. She knew Meredith
wanted to shout after her; she could almost hear her
cousin's teeth snapping together.

Mason and Jordon were talking as Lise entered the
dining-room, still trembling with the shock of Meredith's outburst. Both men rose. Jordon's dark eyes slid
over her in slow masculine appraisal, but she ignored
him.

Ready?' His voice was amused, aware of her

response to him. She angled her head towards him, nodding coolly.

'Enjoy yourselves,' said Mason, still beaming generously.

Lise kissed his cheek and without a word walked stiffly towards the private elevator. She half expected Meredith to be lying in wait for them, but the older girl was nowhere to be seen, and she couldn't help a sigh of relief as the elevator doors closed behind them.

She was thinking that Meredith and Jordon had discussed her, and her heart was clenching with pain. If he forced her to continue with this charade of spending the day with him, she would not say a thing.

'Stop sulking,' said Jordon, laughing.

'I'm not sulking.' She refused to look at him. 'Don't flatter yourself.'

As they reached the foyer, she asked, 'Where are we going?'

He took her arm, his light touch burning her skin, and led her towards his car. 'Wait and see,' he said, with an infuriating smile.

Shrugging, Lise slid into the passenger seat, watching him from beneath her lashes as he walked round the front of the car. She turned her head away, though, as he slid in beside her and started the engine.

She had to remain composed. She had to keep him at a distance, she told herself sternly. And she had to control this trembling weakness, the dangerous excitement that his nearness induced. The way she felt now overwhelmed her with its intensity and left her troubled and confused. Jordon meant more to her than she could bear to admit. Her heart had lifted with a terrible, painful joy when she had turned and found him watching her this morning.

Yet he belonged—if belonged was the right word, if

Jordon would ever belong to anybody—to her cousin. By being with him now, even though the situation was not of her own making, she was causing terrible trouble between Meredith and herself.

She stared out of the car window as they sped down the hill, through the heart of the city, to the shore. The streets were laid out like a chessboard, all perfectly straight, and their progress was slowed by the heavy lunchtime traffic and the numerous intersections of right-angled crossroads.

Jordon took his eyes from the road for a second, and glared at her huddled against the passenger door.

'You're very quiet,' he teased gently.

Lise didn't look at him, still locked in her own pain. 'What do you expect?' she asked tonelessly. 'I didn't want this. You forced——' Meredith's accusing face rose before her and she flinched, the words tailing off.

Jordon was silent, and daring to glance at him, she found his face set, devoid of expression.

She had been unforgivably rude, and already regretted her harsh words. She had been lying too. She wanted to be with him, oh, so much. Perhaps she had only been trying to hurt him because she felt so guilty about Meredith, about her own feelings, about everything. And with a flash of insight, she realised that Jordon knew it, probably even understood. He was a wise, perceptive man.

She looked at the tall buildings, the sunlight falling in long shadows on the crowded pavements. 'Everything is just as I remember,' she said lightly, trying to make amends and end the tense, suffocating silence.

'Glad to be back?' His voice was as light as hers.

'Yes.' There was a second's hesitation that gave her away. In truth, she hadn't really thought of it before. It was wonderful to be reconciled with Mason, but she did miss her life in London, her flat, her work and her friends. Mason wanted her company and that was fine with her, but it did leave her with a lot of time on her hands, something she wasn't used to. Time that was increasingly filled with thoughts of the man beside her. She couldn't hide her sudden despair as she added, 'It doesn't seem as though I've been away for three years.'

They were passing the yacht harbour, she noticed, driving towards the Golden Gate Bridge, and she wondered again where Jordan was taking her. She looked at the tall masts of the boats. There were children playing on the grassy verges, and she shivered involuntarily. Then they were crossing the bridge, the calm Pacific Ocean glinting below them. A blue and gold cruise boat, full of tourists, moved slowly beneath them. The bay cruise was an essential item on any visitor's itinerary, and consequently the boat was filled to capacity.

Once across the bridge, Jordon deftly manoeuvred the car through the traffic, taking the road to Sausalito. Like Lise, he had fallen silent, and she could think of nothing to say. It was better that way, she thought. It prevented her from making a fool of herself.

A short time later they drew up in front of a tall, modern building, constructed entirely of redwood and glass. A painted sign proclaimed the building as 'The Sausalito Theatre Company. Home of the People's Players.'

Jordon glanced at her rapt face as he opened the passenger door and she climbed out. She looked around with interest. It was obvious that a lunchtime performance was about to begin. There were people strolling towards the wide open doors: businessmen in smart suits, well-dressed women, and young people, casually attired.

She allowed Jordon to take her arm, trying to ignore the fierce tingle of awareness that shot through her body.

The theatre was dim and cool inside. It smelled of mellow wood, and flowers and oranges. There was a huge round stage, the seats tiered all around it.

The lunchtime production was based loosely on *King Lear*, and Jordon steered Lise to two of the best seats in the place. He was obviously known here, she thought, her lips tightening with jealousy as she recalled the casual but radiant greeting he had received from the beautiful young girl at the box office. The theatre was full and the play was about to start. Jordon was watching her, his mouth indulgent, and she turned her golden head away, concentrating on the stage in front of them.

Ninety minutes later, they walked out of the theatre into the brilliant sunshine. Lise had enjoyed every second of the play, and her green eyes were sparkling.

The company was brilliant, innovative and sensitive, and their performance had been unusual and exciting. She had heard of them, of course. They had been receiving rave reviews in the *Chronicle* for practically every production they staged. They were going places.

'Hungry?' asked Jordon, smiling at her.

She looked up into his lean hard face and returned the smile, her heart leaping into her throat. 'Ravenous,' she admitted. 'Thank you for bringing me here. I haven't been near a theatre since I arrived.'

'You enjoyed it?'

She watched his mouth as he spoke, heat weakening her lower limbs. 'Very much. It makes me wish——'

She broke off, shrugging.

'What?' he demanded softly.

'Oh, that I was working again.' She moved her hands self-consciously, aware of him with every fibre of her being. All thoughts of the play suddenly faded. She felt as though they were alone in the world, and that made her panic.

'You could be,' said Jordan, his mouth curving as he read her expressive features.

'I don't understand.' She was imagining what his skin felt like. His shirt sleeves were rolled up to the elbow. His forearms were tanned and strong, liberally sprinkled with dark hairs.

'You will.'

The Lion Garden Restaurant was on the seafront in the centre of Sausalito. They were shown to a secluded table on the plant-filled terrace that overlooked the ocean. The waiter fussed around them, and Lise smiled. She was getting used to being treated like royalty whenever she was with Jordon.

Jordon ordered seafood, the restaurant's speciality, and chilled white wine, and as the waiter bustled away, another man approached their table. He was tall and thin with streaked blond hair, and he exuded a nervous energy belied by his wide, easy smile.

He greeted Jordon as a friend, nodding smilingly at Lise, his narrowed eyes running over her swiftly and appreciatively. Jordon made the introductions. 'Lise, this is Victor Jamal, he runs the People's Players. Vic, let me introduce you to Lise Holbrook, a very talented actress, looking for work.'

Lise flushed at the compliment, holding out her hand to Victor Jamal.

Lunch passed in a haze. Lise sipped chilled wine and ate her fill of fresh delicately flavoured lobster.

Jordon and Victor talked about the theatre, arguing lightly and laughing, and Lise was not surprised at Jordon's vast knowledge of the performing arts.

Victor left before coffee was served, shaking Lise's hand firmly. The company was starting rehearsals for a new play within the fortnight. He would send her the script, and she was to call him for an audition, he told her, as soon as she had read it.

Lise thanked him, hardly able to believe her good fortune, and he replied that anybody recommended by Jordon was obviously pretty special. Real talent was thin on the ground.

When he had gone, she turned excitedly to Jordon, and found him watching her expressionlessly. Fragrant coffee was set in front of them by a silent waiter who disappeared as soon as the china cups were on the table.

'You've been so kind,' she said, very seriously. 'I don't know how to thank you.'

'Don't you?' His grey eyes were amused, mocking, and something Jerri had said suddenly flashed into Lise's mind. 'He could do a hell of a lot for your career.'

'I hope you don't think . . .'

'Mmm?'

'What I mean is, I hope you don't think that I . . .' She floundered, totally out of her depth, totally embarrassed.

Jordon laughed, throwing back his dark head. 'I don't,' he said, very amused.

For some reason the words hurt, and Lise flushed scarlet, averting her eyes, watching two men being shown to the table next to theirs.

As they sat down, one of the men was facing her, and as she recognised him suddenly, all the colour seeped out of her face.

Her hand began to shake. Hot coffee spilled on to the heavy linen tablecloth, but she didn't notice. She was too busy trying to pull herself together . . .

Paul Lianos was sitting only a few feet away, and she felt physically sick, her overwhelming desire to run from the room.

She put down her coffee cup with a jarring rattle against its saucer, dragging her eyes away only to meet Jordon's heavy, narrowed stare.

He had seen everything. His eyes were as cold and as hard as steel as they flicked over Paul Lianos, before returning to search Lise's face. His expression was impassive, but she knew that his clever brain was working, trying to assess the situation.

Her breath came sharply into her throat and she lowered her head. Paul Lianos hadn't changed much in three years. His face was still handsome, but it was arrogant and self-satisfied and his eyes were cruel. She saw him clearly for the very first time, and wondered, even though she'd been impossibly innocent then, how she had ever found him attractive.

She looked at him again, and felt very cold inside. Memories were flooding through her brain, unwanted and horrifying. She hated him even now. She would always hate him.

As she looked at him with horror, he became aware of her scrutiny and their eyes met. He stopped talking to his companion, recognition suddenly dawning in his blue eyes. Lifting his glass, he saluted her, smiling with what she read as secret sensual knowledge.

Lise almost shuddered with loathing and froze him with the coldest look in the world, turning her whole body away from him.

Jordon watched the exchange, then stared at Lise, his mouth hard and very angry. Lise couldn't stop shivering. Misery engulfed her, the sweet joy of the day completely lost.

'Excuse me, Mr Hayes.' The head waiter was hovering, his face apologetic, a telephone in his hand. 'A call for you, sir. I wouldn't have disturbed you, but it is, apparently, very urgent.' There was a question in his eyes. 'Will you take it here, or would you prefer to take it in one of the booths?'

Jordon glanced up, his face blank. 'I'll take it here, thank you, Ricardo.' He took the telephone, his eyes still on Lise as he spoke into the receiver.

Lise didn't listen to what he was saying. She stared blindly into his strong face, hardly aware of what she was doing. She was thinking of Paul Lianos, of what he had done to her. For three years she hadn't been able to let a man near her. He had scarred her, body and mind.

'That was Nancy.' Jordon's harsh voice broke into her unpleasant thoughts. 'Mason has had another heart attack.' Lise stared at him blankly, trying to take the news in.

Jordon's mouth tightened impatiently. 'Did you hear what I said?'

She nodded, the sunlight in her hair framing her face with light.

'Is he . . .?' She couldn't complete the question.

'No.' Jordon's voice was gentler, reassuring. He got to his feet in one lithe movement, pulling her up too. 'But we're leaving now. He's asking for you.' His hand closed around her elbow. His fingers hurt her, but Lise didn't care. The pain was almost a relief; it shocked her out of her trance-like state.

She didn't look back at Paul Lianos as she walked out of the restaurant with Jordon, but she was aware that his eyes were following her every inch of the way.

CHAPTER SEVEN

THE ride back to San Francisco was completed in silence. Jordon drove fast; he was a good driver, totally in control of the vehicle. Lise sat beside him, staring out of the windscreen in front of her. She felt numb, devoid of emotion.

She glanced at Jordon once as they shot back across the Golden Gate Bridge. His profile was unyielding, a muscle flicking rhythmically in his jaw. She wondered, vaguely, what he was thinking, before turning back to the road being eaten up in front of them. She had sensed his curiosity about Paul Lianos, and something eLse too. Anger? Dislike? She shook her head, unable to work it out.

When they arrived at the hospital, Jordon slid out of the car, walking swiftly round to help her out. He glanced down at her small pale face, as he led her through the wide, electronically-operated doors. Lise stared back at him, not hiding her fear, her concern for her grandfather. She needed reassurance, but her throat was blocked by a tight knot of emotion and she couldn't speak.

'This way.' He led her into the lift, his light touch on her arm offering her all the strength and comfort she needed. Lise wanted to rest her head against his wide shoulder, and it was only by sheer effort of will that she didn't give in to the impulse.

Mason's private room seemed full of people. A nurse stood by the bedside, monitoring the complicated-looking equipment that lay all around the bed.

Meredith was by the window, sullen and silent. Nancy's face was tight with the effort of not crying. Both looked up as Lise and Jordon entered the room, and, ignoring Meredith's caustic, 'At last!', Lise rushed into Nancy's arms.

'How is he?' she whispered against Nancy's cheek, crying herself, suddenly.

'Stable, for the moment at least,' Nancy replied, her voice choking.

Lise hadn't dared to look at her grandfather, but she looked now. He lay inert against a high bank of pillows. His skin was yellow, filmed with sweat. His eyes flickered as she looked at him, red-rimmed, glazed. His mouth moved without sound as he recognised Lise, his hand lifting weakly from the bedclothes as though to beckon her to him.

She moved close, dashing the tears from her face, trying to smile down at him. His eyes focused on her with difficulty, and she suddenly saw his indomitable strength, his sheer will to live, despite the damnable weakness of his heart.

'Get rid—of everybody,' he managed breathlessly. 'Want to talk—to you.'

Lise looked helplessly at Nancy, who nodded and got to her feet, ushering Meredith and the nursing staff out of the room.

Lise looked round for Jordon, but he had already gone, she didn't know when.

Alone, she looked down at her grandfather. 'You should try to get some rest,' she said gently. 'We can talk when you're stronger.'

'Now,' he asserted, his voice weak, but the will behind it inflexible, and she knew that it was useless to try and stop him.

'You're—you're in love with Jordon Hayes, aren't you?'

Lise closed her eyes, shocked by the question. 'Yes,' she admitted quietly, after a moment. She couldn't lie, even though the truth made her heart ache heavily. Mason nodded, almost smiling.

'Bring him in here,' he said slowly. 'And Nancy.'

'Okay.' Lise stood up and walked out of the room. Jordon was outside, talking to Nancy and the two nurses.

'He's asking for you both,' she said, meeting his grey eyes reluctantly.

Jordon nodded, walking back inside with her, Nancy following. Mason's eyes were closed, his breathing slow and unsteady.

'Grandpa?' she whispered, thinking that if he was asleep, they would leave. But his eyelids opened slowly, and he saw Jordon at her side.

'Good,' he said with difficulty. 'Good.' His eyes rested on Lise. 'I want you to promise—promise me this.' He was getting weaker, Lise could see it, and she was afraid that he would kill himself if he didn't rest soon.

'Anything,' she said desperately, her eyes filling with tears.

Mason's lips stretched into a tired half smile. 'You wouldn't last five minutes in business—agreeing before you know—the terms.'

A spasm of pain crossed his face, and he took a shallow, unsteady breath. It seemed to bring him back to his purpose.

'Marry Jordon,' he said, looking her straight in the eye. 'Marry him now.'

'Grandpa!' Lise's eyes dilated with shock.

Mason cut her off. 'Your mother was a fool—

nothing I could do for her—God knows, the guilt was still there.' His skin seemed to darken, a torment in his eyes. 'I've got nothing now—I might not even make it through this. I want to make sure that you're all right.'

'I will be,' Lise whispered, tears spilling down her face, unchecked, unheeded. 'You mustn't worry, and you don't have to——'

'Jordon——' Mason's face contracted painfully.

'She'll marry me!' Jordon promised, his voice low and hard. 'Won't you, Lise?'

Looking at her grandfather, Lise knew she was defeated. 'Yes', she acknowledged. 'Yes, I'll marry him, if that's what you want. But you must rest now, please!'

'Now—you'll marry him now,' commanded Mason, his voice as thin as wire. 'Nancy—the papers——'

Lise swayed dizzily, aware of Jordon's strong hands steadying her, his touch cutting through everything. It was like a dream, a nightmare.

Jordon took the papers from Nancy, scanning them with narrowed eyes, nodding as he handed them back.

Then, *incredibly*, there was a minister in the room, a gentle-looking man with white hair, and a black collar, who smiled at Lise with kind blue eyes.

'Jordon?' She touched his arm lightly, pleading for his help, but his eyes were cold and blank as he looked down at her, as though he was very angry about something.

'Are you ready?' he enquired, and she shivered at what she saw in those eyes, frightened of him, and knowing suddenly that this had been inevitable from the moment they met. She was trapped. There was absolutely nothing she could do, and her defeat left a bitter taste in her mouth.

'Yes,' she replied, her breath coming sharply. The

feeling that this was all some strange unreal dream persisted through the ceremony.

She listened to Jordon's deep calm voice as he spoke his vows and heard her own voice promising to love and honour until death. Jordon seemed remote, a dark stranger. She didn't know him at all. This can't be happening, she thought, panic rising in her stomach, as Jordon removed a thin gold ring from his finger, sliding it on to hers to seal the marriage. The ring was still warm from his skin, and it felt heavy and alien on her hand. Had it belonged to his wife? she wondered with numb horror, trembling as the service ended and the minister pronounced them man and wife.

Jordon bent his head, his cool mouth touching hers briefly, without tenderness. Lise looked at her grandfather. His eyes were closed, the satisfied ghost of a smile touching the corners of his mouth. For a second, her heart leapt into her throat, until she realised he was sleeping at last, his wish fulfilled. She was grateful for that, at least.

'You really must leave now,' the nurse said briskly. 'Mr Holbrook must be allowed peace and quiet.'

'But he will be—I mean, he——' Lise blurted out, unable to frame the question.

The nurse's eyes softened slightly. 'He's as well as can be expected. I suggest you talk to Dr Salvador, he can put you fully in the picture.'

Lise nodded, thanking her, though not encouraged. Mason wanted everything tied up. Perhaps he didn't expect to live. She found it impossible to believe that he might die; his spirit seemed so strong!

She turned away from Mason to find both Nancy and Jordon watching her.

Nancy smiled. 'I've telephoned the apartment,' she said brightly. 'Everything is being arranged.'

'Arranged?' echoed Lise blankly, as they walked towards the elevator.

Nancy faltered. 'Oh, but I thought—well, I assumed you and Jordon would be leaving almost immediately.'

'We will be,' Jordon cut in, smiling at the older woman. Exuding that fatal charm, Lise thought bitterly. Even Nancy was not immune.

'I'm so happy for you both,' said Nancy, taking Lise's arm. 'Do you know, I *thought* there was something going on between you two!'

Lise flushed, not knowing what to say. Nancy obviously thought the marriage was a love match, not just another of Mason's cunning schemes. She looked up into Jordon's dark face, and saw that his eyes were gleaming with mockery.

'It might not have been the wedding we wanted,' he said blandly to Nancy. 'But it was Mason's wish, and Lise wanted to please him.'

Lise drew a sharp breath, biting back the acid retort that hovered on her tongue. She hadn't had any choice at all. Her eyes flashed fire at him, but he smiled, his mobile mouth twisting with amusement as he led her out into the afternoon sunlight. Nancy walked to Mason's waiting limousine. There was no sign of Meredith; she had disappeared before the ceremony.

In Jordon's car, as they drove back to Nob Hill, Lise fiddled with the gold ring on her finger. It was too big, too heavy. She couldn't believe, even now, that she was married to the man beside her. She touched her tongue to her dry lips as the implications sank in. She turned to Jordon in sudden panic.

'Was that a legal ceremony? Are we really . . .?'

'Married?' Jordon supplied, casting her a dark, narrowed glance. 'Yes, we are.' There was anger in the clipped words, and Lise shrank from it.

'But how?' she whispered, frightened.

'It was arranged some weeks ago. Mason leaves nothing to chance, you should know that by now. This sudden illness just brought the date forward.'

'But what about the blood test?' floundered Lise, grasping at straws. She knew that in the United States this was a necessary formality before a marriage could take place.

Jordon's mouth twisted sardonically. 'Louis Salvador gave you a check up just after you arrived back in San Francisco, didn't he?' His voice mocked her naïvety. 'These things are easy enough to arrange.'

Lise fell silent. So, Mason had arranged it all; he had been plotting away behind her back. How could he? she thought bitterly. He had been pushing her into Jordon's arms from the moment she arrived back, and she had been too stupid to see it, imagining foolishly that he had somehow mellowed in his old age.

'You must have known he wanted us married,' said Jordon, a curious bitterness in his tone.

'It hadn't occurred to me,' she replied numbly, and he laughed.

'Are you really as naïve as you seem, Lise?' he queried softly.

'I suppose I must be.' Defensive anger came to her rescue. She was a fool and she knew it. She didn't need him to rub it in. 'But it doesn't really matter. At least I'm learning my lesson. We'll just have to have this ridiculous marriage annulled.' Her voice came out sharp and cold and very insulting.

The car slowed. They were back at Mason's apartment building.

Jordon turned to her slowly, sliding his tanned arm along the back of her seat, trapping her even though he wasn't touching her. 'Oh, no,' he murmured. 'There will be no annulment, my love.'

Lise's green eyes widened in shock, and he asked mockingly, 'Why are you so surprised?'

'You don't want this . . . any more than I do,' she said, her breath coming quickly. The harsh words held a question. She loved him so desperately, and she needed some small spark of reassurance.

Jordon's cool grey eyes searched hers. 'No,' he responded coldly, 'I don't.'

'Then why won't——?' She felt tears blurring her vision at his cold-hearted indifference. The wide shoulders lifted indolently.

'I want you. I've never made any secret of that.' The words were coolly and evenly spoken, yet the eyes that held hers darkened, burning with a deep fire.

Lise shivered. 'I despise you,' she said fiercely. 'And I won't sleep with you. I won't let you touch me!'

Jordon smiled slightly, his hand reaching lazily to cup her flushed face.

Before she realised his intention, his mouth found hers with a deep, punishing kiss that ground her soft lips against the sharpness of her teeth. She moaned deeply, her own hands coming up to his powerful shoulders to push him away. But he was too strong for her and an unbidden, unwanted response was rising up inside her like a flood-tide, leaving her weak and suddenly passive beneath the hungry pressure of his mouth.

When he finally let her go, her lips were bruised and swollen, her green eyes dazed with deep passion. Jordon looked down into her flushed face with blank intensity, and her heart lurched violently.

'Damn you,' she whispered, her passion turning to angry shame. 'Damn you!'

Nancy had organised an impromptu champagne

lunch for them. Lise was moved by her kindness, but unable to touch any of the tasty delicacies prepared by Mason's staff. She sipped champagne as though it was water. She felt nervous, thirsty, almost as though she had a fever.

'I only wish I'd had the time to organise a proper reception,' Nancy said wistfully. 'Though I expect Jordon will be arranging a wedding party,' she continued, her eyes on the tall, dark-haired man who seemed to dominate the room.

'I don't know.' Lise felt like laughing. She was on the edge of hysteria, her nerves at breaking point.

'And you could take your vows again in church,' Nancy suggested, her eyes misting. 'Much more romantic.'

Lise didn't answer. The thought of a church wedding to a man who didn't love her made her heart ache. She took another sip of champagne.

'It doesn't seem real,' she said, suddenly close to tears.

Nancy smiled, misunderstanding. 'Mason can be so insensitive sometimes,' she said gently. 'Don't be too angry with him.' She took a deep breath, then said. 'He wanted to make sure that your future was secure, just in case. He's carried a terrible burden of guilt about your mother all these years, and the same thing nearly happened with you. He sees himself as a patriarch, it's in his nature to try and run people's lives. I suppose it's true what they say about power corrupting, but he's not a bad man underneath,' She looked into Lise's pale, strained face. 'You are happy, aren't you, darling? You do love Jordon?'

Lise heard the anxiety in Nancy's voice, the sudden fear that perhaps a terrible mistake had been made. Nancy was under an intolerable strain with Mason's illness and the loss of the company, and Lise could't add to it.

She tried to smile. 'Of course I'm happy. You mustn't worry about me.'

'You look so pale.' Nancy stroked back a strand of Lise's blonde hair that had escaped its tortoiseshell comb.

'I can't stop thinking about Grandpa,' Lise admitted.

Nancy shook her head. 'He's in the best possible hands. Louis will take good care of him. You must turn your thoughts to your new husband.'

Lise looked over at Jordon again, and felt that familiar pain in the region of her heart.

Meredith had just entered the room. She had changed into tight black trousers and a loose, fashionable T-shirt that fell casually off one slim, tanned shoulder. Lise watched her walk over to Jordon, murmur something to him that made him smile. Then, standing on her toes, she wound her arms around his neck and kissed his mouth.

Lise drew breath sharply, riveted by that kiss. It seemed to last for ages until Jordon gently but firmly disentangled himself, holding Meredith away from him.

Lise looked away, unbearably hurt, jealousy stabbing at her like a physical pain.

Nancy clucked her tongue disapprovingly. She too had watched what was going on. 'Meredith is such a bad loser,' she said, smiling. 'Angela spoiled her rotten. I think she had designs on Jordon.'

'So do I,' Lise replied, unable to hide her jealousy.

'Too late.' Nancy saw that jealousy and smiled, sure now that Lise really was in love with her new husband. 'He belongs to you.'

Lise's mouth twisted. Jordon belonged to nobody but himself. As she stared at him, he became aware of her gaze, and their eyes met across the room. He smiled at her, eyes gentle, and she lowered her own eyes, desperately lonely.

There was no one she could talk to. Her chance to tell Nancy the truth had passed. She was frightened to death of being alone with Jordon, and she knew the time was drawing near. He didn't love her, she knew that as surely as she knew her own love for him. Mason might have thought he was acting for her benefit, but he had forced her into an intolerable situation.

The light, sure touch on her shoulder made her jump. It seared through the thin material of her blouse, and she turned, aware of the man beside her with every fibre of her being.

He slid his arm around her shoulder, and an intense yearning flared in her. She concentrated on that feeling, dimly aware that he was thanking Nancy for the party, keenly aware that they were about to leave. Her suitcases were standing by the elevator doors; she had seen them on the way in.

Jordon turned to her, his eyes glittering. 'Ready to go?' he enquired softly.

'In a moment.' She fled from the room in panic, playing for time, seeking the sanctuary of her bedroom for the last time. It seemed empty, despite the luxurious décor. Leaving the door wide open, she walked over to the windows, staring out across the city below, her arms wrapped protectively around her body. So much had happened in the last twelve hours. The theatre company and the chance of work, Paul Lianos, Mason's heart attack, and most incredible of all, the marriage ceremony at her grandfather's bedside.

Soon, she would be alone with the man she loved more than life itself. The thought terrified her.

A movement outside the door registered in the corner of her eye.

'Meredith?' she called, wanting a word with her cousin, hoping, if not to put things right, then at least ease the situation bstween them before she left.

Meredith retraced her steps, coming into Lise's bedroom and closing the door. Her eyes were hard and unfriendly. 'Yes?' she demanded contemptuously. 'What is it?'

Lise lifted her shoulders inadequately. 'I don't know where to start,' she said hopelessly.

Meredith's smile was spiteful. She said nothing, and Lise had to struggle on. 'I—well, I know how all this must look,' she began with difficulty.

'What can you mean?' Meredith cut in sarcastically, enjoying Lise's embarrassment. Beneath her smile there was dislike and contempt, and Lise shrank from it.

'You know what I mean,' she said quietly. 'Jordon. This morning you accused me of running after him . . .'

'And this afternoon, I find that you've married him. Fast work, Lise, you must know every trick in the book,' replied Meredith. 'It seems to me that you're nothing more than a high class slut. Like mother, like daughter, I suppose.'

Lise paled at the insult. 'Meredith, please! I know how you must feel——'

'Do you? Do you really? Do you think I'm interested in your explanations? Let me tell you, I'm not!' Her cousin's eyes glittered with malice. 'I wish you all the luck in the world—you're going to need it!'

'I'm sorry.' Lise had been clumsy, too anxious to try to explain. If Meredith loved Jordon, Mason's manipulations must have hurt her terribly.

'Oh, you will be,' Meredith promised, a bitter hatred twisting her face. 'It's all so bloody civilised, isn't it?' She turned, pacing the pale carpet. 'Mason has got someone else lined up for me now, did you know that?'

'No!' Lise was shocked.

'He's very eligible, very handsome, and I'm going to marry him, as planned. Dear Mason has it all worked out.'

'Do you love him?' Lise asked tentatively, realising for the first time the full extent of Mason's ruthlessness. How many people's lives had he ruined with his manipulations, his greed for power?

'Love?' Meredith echoed the word as though she had never heard it before. 'Who cares about love? I want money and power. If it hadn't been for Mason, and you, Jordon would have married me, and I wouldn't have been cheated out of what is rightfully mine.'

'Mason's fortune,' said Lise slowly, everything suddenly clear.

Meredith stared at her with wild eyes. 'How sanctimonious you are,' she said, with chilling anger. 'So sweet and innocent, so worried about Mason. He's cut you out of his will, did you know that? I expect you did—Nancy was always very fond of you. I was going to get everything, provided I toed the line, and I was more than willing to do that. I had no intention of letting what happened to my mother happen to me. Mason ruined her life, and I'll never forgive him for that. I hope he dies!'

'Don't!' Meredith's bitterness was frightening. Lise took a step away, but Meredith gripped her arm, hurting her.

'Oh, no. You're going to listen to every word I've got to say to you, you sly little bitch. If only Mason hadn't had that first heart attack, you wouldn't have come back here; Jordon would have been mine.'

'You're in love with him, aren't you?' whispered Lise painfully, imagining that that was why Meredith was so upset. Meredith's answer surprised her.

'No, love is for sentimental fools like you, but Jordon is everything I could want in a man. When he takes over Holbrook International, he'll be the most powerful man in San Francisco. He'll have more money than Mason ever had.' She paused, her blue eyes gleaming. 'And of course, he's fantastic in bed.'

Lise flinched, and Meredith laughed. 'You can't take it, can you? I'm glad I'm going be here to watch you disintegrate. What does it feel like to be married to a man who doesn't give a damn about you? How does it feel to know that your infatuation amuses him? He'll use you until he tires of you, and that shouldn't be long.'

'For God's sake——' Lise tried to pull away, her body freezing cold, but Meredith still held her arm in a paralysing grip, and she couldn't free herself.

'How does it feel to know that you've been bought, Lise?' The voice was taunting, and Lise stiffened.

'What do you mean?'

'Jordon hasn't mentioned it?' Meredith laughed spitefully. 'You fool! Surely you don't imagine he married you because he wanted to?'

Lise closed her eyes. She didn't want Meredith to know just how much this dreadful conversation was affecting her. So much for being an actress, she thought bitterly. Meredith was reading her like a book, knowing just how to cause the maximum pain.

'I don't know,' she said wearily, aware that Meredith was watching, waiting for an answer. A feeling of icy foreboding was settling over her.

'Well, let me enlighten you. Jordon gets Holbrook International, but he has to take you as part of the deal—Mason's ridiculous conscience raising its ugly head, I suppose. Jordon has been after the company for years. Mason may be in trouble after that fiasco in the Far East, but he's still got bargaining power. I heard them talking on the telephone. It was all sewn up weeks ago.' Her expression was vicious and triumphant.

Lise felt sick. She didn't want to believe it, but somewhere inside, she knew that it was true. She knew Mason. At the hospital, he had practically admitted what Meredith was saying. It was history repeating itself.

Meredith released her arm, staring with satisfaction at the red marks on Lise's skin. She pushed back her hair and walked towards the bedroom door.

'Good luck, dear cousin,' she said, still smiling. 'And you can't imagine how much pleasure it gives me to know that you're going to need it.'

CHAPTER EIGHT

JORDON'S house was high in the hills of Marin County, not far from the National Monument of Muir Woods. It was a huge, rambling house, constructed of stone and mellow redwood, hidden from view by a thick belt of trees.

Before reaching the house, the car pulled through high, electronically-operated wrought iron gates, watched over by two unwinking video cameras, and then glided along a twisting drive edged with pine, eucalyptus and redwood trees.

The house itself was built on two levels, with wide wooden verandas running along both floors. It was a new house, modern in design, and every window afforded a panoramic view of tall trees, greenery and peaceful tranquillity. It was a wonderful place to live—Lise could appreciate that even though she felt overwhelmed by her own misery. At any other time she would have been eager to explore what lay behind the many polished wooden doors, but Meredith's cruel words lingered in her mind.

Jordon led her into a beautifully furnished living-room. He seemed aware of her silent withdrawal, his narrowed eyes searching her face as she blankly took in her new surroundings.

It was a large, square room, decorated in creamy white and very pale delphinium blue. Floor-length white curtains screened the long windows, and thickly patterned rugs lay on the floor. The sofas were white, scattered with inviting-looking blue and white cushions. The paintings that lined the panelled walls were by contemporary artists—paintings of the West Coast, in startling shades of blue.

A knock on the door heralded the arrival of Jordon's housekeeper, Mrs Porter. Jordon made the introductions, explaining that Mrs Porter and her family lived in a separate house in the grounds, Mr Porter attending to the gardens and the pool.

Lise smiled, taking an instant liking to the middle-aged woman with kind eyes who was assessing her from head to toe and nodding her approval.

'Congratulations to you both,' Mrs Porter said enthusiastically. 'I've arranged for your cases to be sent upstairs, and in the meantime, is there anything I can fetch for you, Mrs Hayes?'

Lise felt her heart pounding. Mrs Hayes! Would she ever get used to being called that?

'Some coffee would be lovely,' she managed, her green eyes mirroring her shock.

Mrs Porter nodded, her smile wide. 'Mr Hayes?' She turned to Jordon, who was watching Lise, easily reading her expressive features.

'I think I need something a little stronger,' he drawled with a dry smile. 'After you've brought the coffee for my wife, perhaps you would take the rest of the week off.'

Mrs Porter's eyes glowed with understanding. 'Thank you, sir, you're very kind.'

She left the room, but was back in a matter of moments carrying a large silver tray, laden with tiny, delicious-looking sandwiches and a tall pot of aromatic coffee. Lise thanked her, and as Jordon exchanged a few words with the housekeeper before her departure, Lise moved over to the windows, staring out at the profusion of flowers and trees.

Apprehension was gnawing away inside her. When Mrs Porter left they would be alone in this beautiful house. She wasn't sure what Jordon expected of her, but she was suddenly afraid. The knowledge that he had married her because he wanted Holbook International lay heavily in her heart.

Fool, she chided herself. How could it have been any other way? Why did you have to fall in love with him?

'Shall I pour your coffee?' Jordon's husky voice made her jump.

She turned and met his glance with wide dark eyes.

'This ring.' She held up her hand, voicing the question that had been nagging away at her for hours. 'Did . . . did it belong to your wife?'

'Would it worry you if it had?' He walked over to a tray of drinks, conveniently situated on a low, white occasional table, and poured himself a measure of Bourbon, raising it to his lips with a mocking salute before draining the glass.

Lise watched the indolent grace of his movements, unable to drag her hungry eyes away.

'Did it?' she repeated tremulously.

'It belonged to my mother,' Jordon revealed softly.

'Oh.' Feeling foolish for making such an issue of it, though she couldn't deny the relief his answer gave her, she busied herself with the tray of coffee, trying to conceal the shaking of her hands as she sipped the hot liquid.

'If it bothers you, I'll buy you a wedding ring,' said Jordon watching her.

'It doesn't matter,' she replied, embarrassed.

'It seemed to a minute ago.'

She frowned. 'I . . . Tell me about your wife,' she said, changing the subject, not understanding what he was getting at.

'Why are you so interested? It was a long time ago.' He seemed bored by the subject. How could she tell him that she was consumed with curiosity about the woman he had loved, perhaps because she knew that she herself would never have his love.

'You were in love with her,' said Lise honestly, finding that she couldn't lie.

'I was young and impatient,' he replied with a smile. 'I didn't know what love was at that age.'

A heavy tension seemed to fill the room. The silence between them deepened, becoming so deep that Lise's nerves were set on edge.

'Oh, this is ridiculous!' she cried at last, jumping to her feet, knocking over her coffee cup in her panic, so that it clattered noisily.

'What is ridiculous?' asked Jordan sardonically.

'I won't stay here!' she said fiercely. 'I won't be tied to you for the rest of my life.'

She walked towards the door, but Jordan caught her before she had time to turn the handle. His hands closed around her upper arm in a grip as hard and as unyielding as steel.

'I'm glad you realise that it's for life,' he told her with cruel amusement, holding her still with consummate ease.

Lise's heart missed a beat. 'You can't keep me here against my will,' she told him, her voice trembling with tears.

The dark brows lifted. 'Perhaps it won't be against your will.' His grey eyes narrowed on the parted softness of her mouth, his meaning clear.

Lise flinched, her face whitening. Of course, he knew that she loved him. She had given herself away so many times. He and Meredith had talked about it, laughed about it.

'I hate you,' she said bitterly, her humiliation crystallising into an anger so fierce that it leapt from her eyes like fire. 'And if you lay a finger on me, I'll kill you, I swear!'

Jordon smiled, a lazy sensuality in the twist of his mouth. 'You have eyes like a cat,' he said softly, still holding her.

'I have claws, too,' Lise informed him wildly. 'And I'll scratch your eyes out if you touch me.'

'Show me,' invited Jordon, laughter in his voice.

He bent his dark head, his mouth finding hers. He kissed her deeply, sweetly, showing her just how sensual a kiss could be.

Lise trembled beneath his mouth, desire piercing her body with a force that left her weak, swaying against him, all anger and hurt pride forgotten. How could she fight, when she wanted him so badly? When Jordon finally released her, she stared up into his dark eyes, her mouth quivering.

'You're my wife, Lise,' he told her. 'And I want you!'

'No,' she protested weakly. 'I'm not your wife, I——'

He took her left hand, lifting it. 'What's this, then?' he demanded quietly, forcing her to look at the gold band that branded her as his possession.

'A joke,' she responded bitterly. 'No, a business deal. The joke is on me.'

'What the hell do you mean?' His hands stilled against her shoulders.

'I mean, that I'm not the fool you take me for. I know all about the deal you made with Mason,' she cried triumphantly.

There was silence. He looked down at her, his face

blank, his hard eyes unreadable.

'It's despicable!' she flung at him, his silence unnerving her. She wanted to hurt him, she wanted to get her own back. 'You're despicable!'

'Who told you?' Jordon demanded, his mouth hardening at her insults. 'Mason?'

Lise's heart clenched with pain. So what Meredith had told her was true. Some tiny part of her had been hoping all this time, refusing to believe it. But Jordon was admitting it now, uncaringly, and she felt as though she wanted to die.

'It doesn't matter who told me,' she said heavily. 'It's enough that I know. I won't sleep with you, not ever. You may have bought Holbrook International, but you haven't bought me!'

'Haven't I?' His voice was hard, each word cold and clear. 'It's time you came to terms with the fact that we're husband and wife—for whatever reason. It's a real marriage, not some platonic adolescent ritual, and I want you in my bed tonight.'

His strong hands pulled her closer, so that she could feel his body, hard and muscular against hers. She was fiercely aware of his strength.

'No,' she whispered, struggling between his hands. 'I can't, not without love,'

Something flickered deep in his cool, silvery glance, then it was gone.

'You can,' he asserted softly. 'And you will.'

One tanned hand slid upwards from her waist to her breast. Lise trembled violently, knowing that beneath the thin cotton of her blouse, Jordon felt the betraying hardness of her nipple.

'Why?' she murmured, defeated, tired of fighting herself as well as him.

'I've never hidden my desire for you,' he told her

deeply, his breath cool against her hair. 'You're going to have to act as my wife, Lise. You've left it too late to change things. It will be much easier if you really are my wife.' He paused. 'In every sense of the word.'

'I'm an actress,' she said acidly. 'Remember?'

Jordon laughed. 'Start learning your rôle, then,' he suggested with unbearable mockery.

As though he had all the time in the world, he took her pointed face between his hands, searching her pleading eyes before closing each eyelid with a kiss.

'You bastard,' she muttered brokenly, but the words were taken from her as his cool mouth touched hers. Now the kiss was angry, ferocious in its intensity. Trembling, Lise kept her lips closed in a hard, stubborn line. His anger scared her. She had gone too far, perhaps deliberately, and suddenly he was cruel and implacable, determined to make her submit to him.

'Open your mouth,' he ordered harshly. 'Haven't you learned yet how to please a man?'

'Obviously not,' she replied, hurt, her sweet breath mingling erotically with his. Jordon took the opportunity to explore the inner softness of her mouth. Desire ached in Lise's breasts, in the contractions of her stomach, an intolerable need shuddering inside her.

'Then it's time you learned,' he drawled huskily, lifting her into his arms as though she were no lighter than a feather.

He carried her up the carved oak staircase, his eyes never leaving her flushed face. She felt the strength of his arms beneath her, the tension of powerful muscles, the deep, steady thud of his heart under her cheek.

She should fight, she thought dazedly, scream, hit him, make him release her somehow, but her eyes were fixed on the strong line of his mouth. It promised expertise, tenderness and strength, everything she needed to assuage the almost physical pain inside her. She was hypnotised by her own need, by his desire, by his very nearness, and she couldn't even protest.

'Jordon,' she whispered in panic, as he carried her towards an arched wooden door which she realised led to his bedroom.

'Be quiet, Lise,' he said smilingly, his glittering eyes holding hers, taking her breath away.

She put her hands up to his wide shoulders, feeling the muscles tensing involuntarily beneath her tentative fingers. It was what she wanted. It was as inevitable as their marriage. Jordon knew that too, she could see it in his dark grey eyes, though she could see no love there.

He kicked shut the bedroom door as he carried her inside. The pale walls of the room were glowing in the late afternoon sunlight. The tall windows stood open, the warm air, birdsong and the scent of flowers drifting into the room.

He carried her to the enormous bed, laying her down gently, arching over her so that his powerful shoulders blocked out the shafts of sunlight that lay in pools on the silk coverlet.

His mouth brushed hers, briefly, hungrily, then moved to her chin, to the sensitive white skin of her throat. Lise could offer no resistance. Her head tilted back helplessly, she shivered as his mouth grazed her neck and shoulders. His lips burned her skin, igniting answering flames in her flesh.

He undressed her quickly, his hard brown hands deft and sure, so that she lay naked, with the cool silk beneath her heated skin.

Then he leant back, his glittering gaze roaming her pale body, imposing possession. Lise flushed scarlet to the roots of her hair, moving to cover herself with her hands. He was still fully clothed, a fact she found disturbingly erotic, because she had never felt more naked.

Jordon smiled, a peculiar tenderness in the smoky depths of his eyes. He took her hands in his own, moving them gently, bending his dark head to kiss each palm, exposing her nakedness again.

'You're beautiful, Lise,' he said huskily. 'So beautiful. I feel as though I've waited——' He broke off, and she gazed into his shadowed eyes, before his mouth parted hers again.

He pressed her down into the softness of the bed. She could feel the breeze blowing gently in her loosened hair.

Jordon's hands were moving against the silk of her skin, tracing the curves from shoulder to thigh, caressing her breasts, her stomach, her hips. She arched against him, gasping with pleasure. His touch was gentle, very sensual. Nothing in her life had prepared her for the intensity of the desire that filled her. She lifted her hands, sliding them around his neck, to twist her fingers in his thick black hair.

The world was blotted out, her mind blank except for the shattering awareness of the man who was making love to her. The kiss went on for ever, deeply intimate and demanding. She could sense Jordon's impatience, she could feel the intolerable need tautening his body, and knew that he was reining it, holding back while he aroused her thoroughly, giving her pleasure before taking his own. The knowledge excited her. She framed the hard bones of his face between her hands, responding with abandon to his searching mouth. With a groan, he raised his head, rolling on to his back to pull his shirt free, shrugging it from his wide shoulders.

Lise watched, so aroused she could hardly bear him to move away from her. His chest was hard and deeply muscled, matted with fine dark hair that arrowed down beneath the belt of his jeans. His skin was smooth and tanned, and she ached to feel its warm texture beneath her fingers.

As he discarded his shirt, she moved so that she was looking down at him, lowering herself deliberately against his bare chest, until his hand came up to curve around the nape of her neck, forcing her mouth down to his once more.

He moved, so that she lay beneath him again, his mouth touching her breasts, his tongue flicking teasingly against her aching nipples. Lise, groaning, arched convulsively against him, her hands holding his dark head to her, betraying her need.

As his mouth moved lower, touching the most intimate parts of her body, she became aware of incredible sensations inside herself, feelings she hadn't imagined existed.

'Jordon,' she whispered, reaching blindly for his muscled shoulders. He was naked, she realised, as the roughness of his thigh touched hers.

'No,' she protested in shock. 'I can't ... I've never...'

He stilled her panic, kissing her mouth tenderly. 'I know. It's all right, my love. I won't hurt you,' he promised, his voice uneven.

'Please, Jordon.' She wanted to fight, but she was dominated, body and soul by the hard muscled body of this man who was her husband. They might have been alone in the world. He held her captive, not by force, but by the sheer magnetism of his presence.

'Touch me,' he commanded raggedly. 'Hold me.

Don't make me take you, Lise. Give yourself to me.'

She listened to his voice end trembled uncontrollably. Of their own volition, her hands touched his chest. The dark mat of hair was springy beneath her fingers. His skin was firm and smooth, lightly filmed with sweat. His heart was pounding heavily. She lost herself in the pleasure of caressing him, of exploring the hard strength of his body, and heard him groan as though he was in agony.

The intensity of his mouth as he reached for her drove all coherent thought from her mind. Within seconds she was unaware of anything but the need to give herself to him, to satisfy the hard thrust of his powerful body.

He took her at last, their bodies fusing hungrily, and the hot aching tension exploded into a rapture beyond belief. She clung to him, crying out his name, her nails raking his smooth shoulders as he brought her slowly and patiently to that moment of shattering, ecstatic release.

It was dark when she woke. She opened her eyes, not knowing where she was for a moment, until the languorous satisfaction of her body brought memory flooding back. She turned her head and found that Jordon had gone. She was alone in the enormous bed, only the indentation on the pillow next to hers and the disarray of the silk sheets evidence of their passionate lovemaking.

She stretched, a lazy smile curving her lips, It had been a devastating experience. Perhaps, she wished for a moment, the naked passion they had shared would enable them to understand each other better.

She slid out of bed, wondering what time it was. The breeze from the open windows was still warm, though the sky was black, twinkling with a million stars.

Uncaring of her nakedness, she walked out on to the tiled balcony, stretching her arms high above her head.

The balcony was lined with terracotta pots of flowers and there was a cane table and chairs just outside the window. The trees rusted mysteriously, and far away, on the top of a distant hill, she could see the lights of a car.

Glancing down at her body, she felt a treacherous weakness in her stomach as she remembered Jordon's mouth against her skin. Her instincts had been right. He was an expert lover, sure and skilful. Her brow creased. How many other women had lain in his arms, begging for his possession as she herself had? The answer came immediately. His experience spoke for itself. Her ridiculous elation faded beneath a tearing jealousy.

Jordon didn't love her; he had already admitted that their marriage was part of the deal for Holbrook International. Knowing that, how could she have allowed him to make love to her? Tears gathered behind her eyes. She had been so definite in her mind that she wouldn't let him touch her. Then she had melted into his arms, unable to resist the powerful magic of his desire. It couldn't have meant any more to him than the satisfaction of his needs, whereas it had changed her for ever. Part of her would always remember this first time, part of her would always belong to him.

She walked back into the bedroom, reaching for a silk wrap that lay across the end of the bed. She felt nothing but disgust at her own weakness. Jordon was as hard as steel, he rode roughshod over anybody who got in his way. How could she be so deeply in love with him?

Snapping on the light switch at the head of the bed, she wondered where she might find her clothes. She could see no sign of her suitcases. With unwilling interest, she looked around the room. The huge bed was the only item of furniture. The floor and ceiling were constructed of pale slats of cedarwood and the drifting curtains, pulled back at the window, were rough silk. The stark simplicity of the room held an unexpected sensuality; the silk-covered bed beckoned, inviting love.

Two adjacent doors, almost invisible on the pale walls, revealed a luxurious en-suite bathroom, and a walk-in dressing-room furnished in dark mahogany. She glanced inside one of the built-in wardrobes, only to find Jordon's clothes. She touched a dark grey suit, her heart aching. How could she stay here? How could she stay with a man who didn't love her? Suddenly it was all too much to bear, and she sank into one of the deeply upholstered chairs in the dressing-room and cried her eyes out.

Later, when she was calm again, empty of tears and determined to be resolute, she washed her face, carefully ignoring her reflection in the mirror, then padded downstairs in search of her suitcases and some clothes.

The lights were on in the living-room and she walked in to find Jordon staring out of the windows, his wide shoulders strangely tense, a glass of Bourbon in his hand.

She watched him for a moment, caught by the sheer masculine beauty of his body, trapped by her love, her desire for him even now. He was wearing faded denim jeans, his muscled torso bare.

Sweet-smelling logs were crackling noisily in the fireplace, their flickering light reflected on the smooth, tanned sweep of his back. He seemed remote, very alone, as though his thoughts troubled him.

Lise's heart turned over. She wanted to run over to him, slide her arms around him and soothe whatever troubled him. She wanted to beg him to make love to her again, but the knowledge that he would reject any show of sympathy held her still and desolate.

Then, as though sensing her presence, he turned slowly and found her watching him. The eyes that met hers were cool and expressionless, and his mouth was unbearably mocking as he raised the glass to his lips and drained the contents in one mouthful.

Her glance wavered and fell to the powerfully muscled lines of his shoulders. She had been mistaken. He was, as ever, in complete command of himself, watching her now as though nothing in the world could touch him.

'So,' he said with a slow smile. 'You're awake at last.' His eyes moved over her slowly. Her body was clearly visible beneath the thin silk wrap and Lise flushed hotly at his dark appraisal.

'I . . . I was wondering where I might find my clothes,' she said, her voice sharp, hating her own embarrassment, hating the knowledge his eyes held.

Jordon watched the graceful tilt of her head and frowned.

'Your suitcases were taken upstairs,' he said quietly. Mrs Porter will have unpacked them for you. Did you look in the dressing-room?'

Unreasonably, the quiet calmness of his voice made Lise's teeth snap together.

'I thought——' She broke off, aware that she had only looked behind one of the wardrobe doors.

Perhaps her clothes were in there. The thought was disturbingly intimate.

'What?' He was still staring, though she couldn't read his expression.

'Nothing. Could I have a drink, please?' His mouth tightened at her withdrawal, but he nodded. 'What would you like?'

'Whisky.' She hardly ever touched spirit but at that moment she was desperate for something that would burn her throat and calm the nerves fluttering in her stomach.

Jordon showed no surprise at her request, moving to pour her a large measure of Scotch.

Lise's eyes followed him, and as he turned his back she suddenly saw the scratches on his shoulders, deep red scars that testified to the primitive abandon she had displayed in his arms.

'Oh, God!' she whispered, horrified.

Jordon's head jerked round, the light catching in his black hair. He saw the direction of her appalled glance and laughed, walking towards her, a glass curved between his strong hands.

'Did I do that?' she asked, staring into his watchful grey eyes.

'I'm flattered,' he said, smiling ironically.

'And I'm sorry.' Lise shifted her eyes, staring at the dark hair on his chest.

She took the glass he offered and sipped the whisky as though it was water. She watched the steady rise and fall of his chest as he breathed and, to her shame, felt fierce desire aching into life in her stomach. The urge to reach out her hand and touch him was almost irresistible, and her fingers tightened around the glass until her knuckles gleamed white.

'What time is it?' she asked when she felt in control

of herself again.

'Nine-thirty.' He didn't move. They were only inches apart, and Lise found herself unable to walk away.

'I'd like to call the hospital.' She could feel the familiar tension stretching between them, electric and powerful. The air was heavy with all that had been left unsaid. She knew that he was watching her, that he would wait for however long it took.

'I've already called,' he told her.

'How is he?'

'Resting. He's still very weak, but they think he'll pull through.'

It was a great relief and it showed in her face. She put down her glass and found the strength to walk away from him.

She had only taken a few steps when his fingers closed around her arm, and he pulled her round to face him.

'We've got to talk,' he said, a muscle flicking tautly in his jaw.

Lise tried to pull free, but his grip tightened, not hurting her, but warning that if she moved, she would be bruised.

'We've nothing to say to each other,' she replied angrily, giving up the struggle but resenting it. 'I won't stay with you! I won't tolerate this fiasco of a marriage! It's loveless and worthless, and ... and I won't stay, do you hear me?' Her voice was high and hysterical, almost out of control.

Jordon's fingers tightened, hurting her now. A shutter came down behind his eyes, so that his expression was ominously blank. 'You'll stay,' he told her in a hard, certain voice. 'You agreed to the marriage, you promised Mason. You had your chance and you didn't take it. If I allowed you to leave, where would you go?'

'It's none of your damned business!' she retorted, feeling as though he had stripped away her skin, leaving her raw and very vulnerable.

He knew very well that he and Mason had manoeuvred her into a corner, that she had nowhere to go. Except perhaps, back to England ... The idea gripped her, until she realised that she couldn't possibly leave San Francisco until she knew for certain that Mason was going to recover.

'You're my wife,' Jordon reminded her again. 'I'd say that made it my business, wouldn't you?'

Looking up into his lean, dark face, the depth of her love for him hit her like a physical blow. She didn't even know if she had the strength to walk away from him.

'Very well, then,' she said, her face hardening. 'What do you suggest?'

Jordon smiled grimly. 'Very calm,' he noted mockingly.

'Why not? I'm sure it won't be difficult to come to some sort of ... arrangement.' She tried to inject just the right amount of boredom into her voice.

The dark brows lifted. 'It's too late, Lise,' he murmured softly.

'I don't understand ...'

'You behaved with beautiful abandon in my arms not so long ago; you can't pretend indifference now.'

Her green eyes widened with shock. 'You may be able to arouse me physically,' she retorted angrily, 'but that doesn't mean I like you!'

'It's a start.' He smiled, his hands gently pulling open the silk wrap. He bent his head, kissing her throat with lingering slowness, his hands sliding up to cup her breasts.

Lise shuddered, her breath coming quickly, desire roaring in her blood.

'No——' she cried, pulling away, finding her strength in the knowledge that he was touching her without desire, deliberately showing her his mastery of her body.

Jordon let her go, watching as she pulled the wrap closed and folded her arms defensively across her breasts.

'You see?' he drawled softly. 'Sexually we're perfectly suited. There's no reason why this marriage shouldn't work.'

'What about love?' Lise whispered painfully.

'What about it? Are you telling me that everything would be fine if I told you that I loved you?' he asked with hard cynicism.

'*No*! No, of course not.' Pain seared her, and she closed her eyes. He wouldn't let her go. He wanted Holbrook International and he was willing to pay the price.

'So what's the problem, then?'

'The problem is that I despise you!' she retorted, pushed beyond anger by his cruelty, uncaring of what she was saying.

His mouth hardened coldly. 'You're beginning to sound like a cracked record.'

He reached out, pulling her hard against his body. His kiss bruised her lips and his arms held her like bands of steel.

She fought like a wildcat for a moment, twisting futilely against the roughness of his bare chest, then suddenly, she was responding mindlessly, her mouth opening beneath his, her hands sliding caressingly to the smooth strength of his shoulders.

Jordon groaned against her lips. His fingers tangled in her hair, pulling back her head to expose the vulnerable line of her throat to his hungry mouth.

He pushed the wrap from her shoulders, fondling her skin, still holding her tightly so that she could feel the hardness of his thighs, the heat of his arousal.

The telephone began to ring, echoing far too loudly in the silent room. Lise jumped as it penetrated her dizzy mind, its intrusion bringing her back to her senses like a douche of cold water.

Jordon lifted his head reluctantly from her naked breasts. 'Leave it,' he suggested thickly, holding her waist between his hands.

'No!' In a panic, she reached out and picked up the receiver before he could stop her.

'Lise?' The deep voice on the other end was instantly recognisable, and the colour drained from her face, her fingers clenching round the telephone. It was Paul Lianos.

'How did you get this number?' she demanded coldly.

'Meredith,' he revealed with amusement. 'Have lunch with me tomorrow.'

Lise felt herself trembling. She couldn't believe his audacity. He was so confident, so sure of himself. She despised him.

'No,' she replied stiffly, and felt Jordon moving. His eyes were fixed on her revealing face, his mouth a hard line.

'Come on,' Paul Lianos said persuasively. 'I couldn't believe my eyes when I saw you today. God, you were beautiful at eighteen, but now you're ravishing!'

Lise listened to the greedy excitement in his voice and nausea rose in her stomach. She drew a long, painful breath, gasping as Jordon suddenly took the receiver from her shaking hand. Without bothering to lift it to his ear, he slammed it back violently in its cradle, cutting the conversation off dead.

Feeling deathly cold, Lise clutched the silk wrap around her throat, staring into his furious face.

'The guy in the restaurant?' he hazarded perceptively.

She nodded. She could feel his anger reaching out, threatening her.

'Was he the reason you left San Francisco?' The question hit her like gunfire.

'Yes.'

'Who is he?'

'Paul Lianos,' she managed through dry lips, hating even saying the words. Jordon nodded, as though the name was familiar to him. 'And what does he mean to you?' he demanded heavily.

'Nothing,' she whispered in sick disgust, turning her head away. She would never be able to tell him the truth. She could imagine how he would look at her if he knew.

Jordon pulled her head round to face him. 'Don't lie to me! I saw the way you reacted to him today. I've never seen you react to any man like that.'

His fingers bit into the soft skin of her jaw. His eyes were as cold as ice, flaying her. 'Are you in love with him?'

Lise couldn't stand it any longer. She wrenched herself away from him, disgust glittering wildly in her eyes.

'Leave me alone!' she shouted at him, and turning on her heel, ran from the room.

CHAPTER NINE

LISE was lying by the pool. She swam every morning, lengths and lengths until she felt pleasantly exhausted, then she climbed out and sunbathed until lunch.

It was a routine she had made for herself, one that she would have enjoyed if she hadn't been feeling so miserable.

She rolled on to her back, stretching lazily on the brightly striped sun lounger, and opened her eyes. She had been here for a week now and the situation between Jordon and herself hadn't improved. If anything, it had worsened since Paul Lianos' inopportune telephone call.

She closed her eyes again. The sun beat down, an orange glare behind her eyelids. It was so peaceful here, she thought, listening to the chattering of the birds, the swift buzz of insects that flew from plant to plant.

At least she hadn't heard from Paul Lianos since that telephone call. She could only hope and pray that she never would again.

The large swimming pool was sited at the back of the house, shaded by a circle of tall old redwood trees. The area around the pool was paved with diamond-shaped terracotta tiles, liberally dotted with comfortable wooden sun loungers and pots of sweet-smelling flowers. A vine and bougainvillaea covered pergola housed a table and chairs for dining outside, and a little way beyond, screened by flowering bushes, there

153

was a sauna and jacuzzi.

There was a peaceful rustic atmosphere, despite the opulent luxury, and Lise had to admit to herself that she had fallen in love with the huge, rambling house and the gardens.

She shifted slightly as the sun began to burn her shoulder, her thoughts turning to Jordon.

She had woken in the grey light of dawn this morning, feeling the deep rhythm of Jordon's heart beneath her cheek. He had been holding her, and she moved closer to him, sliding her arm around his waist, breathing in the clean male scent of his skin. And although it was only an illusion, she had felt she belonged in his arms. She had felt secure for the first time in years.

His strong arms were a shelter in the darkness—protection and comfort. He might not love her, but she needed him, loved him with all her heart. She couldn't deny it any more. She needed his lovemaking, the security and confidence his presence gave her. Her pride lay in the dust. She was willing to take anything he would give her.

He had woken as she clung to him, looking down at her through narrowed eyes. Lise had smiled, still half asleep, her heart in her eyes, and he had bent his dark head and kissed her mouth very gently.

She remembered that kiss now, her face flushing. He had offered her only desire in the past week. That kiss had held the tenderness she craved for. It lingered in her mind, elusive and enchanting.

She had woken later in the morning and he had already gone.

The days had passed quickly since their wedding. Jordon worked in the city all day, then in the evenings they would dine together.

Frightened of giving herself away, Lise was cold and uncooperative when they talked, despite Jordon's efforts to draw her out. Sometimes, after dinner, they would listen to music, and Lise would dream to herself, unaware of Jordon's dark, brooding gaze. Occasionally they played backgammon. Jordon always won. He played with lazy determination and she was no match for his skill. Late in the night, he would reach for her, his mouth hungry, his hands strong, offering her the passion she needed. He would carry her upstairs in his arms, and make love to her in the cool darkness until she was clinging to him, mindlessly begging for his possession.

Her emotions were in turmoil. She knew she should resist when he made love to her, but her desire was stronger than her resolve. The fact that he did not love her made her burn with sad resentment. She hated the cold, ruthless side of his character. It was true that the line between love and hate was very thin; there were times when she wanted to kill him. And there were times when she was so glad to be with him. He respected her as an equal. He admired her intelligence as well as her beauty, and that pleased her. She grabbed at every compliment, hating herself but unable to stop.

She didn't know what would happen to them. She didn't dare to look to the future, even though the present seemed like a kind of limbo. In her mind there was the thought that when Mason recovered, she would leave and go back to England. There was also the hope that Jordon would fall in love with her, and that everything would turn out happily.

She was a fool and she knew it. Jordon never

allowed her to cherish the illusion that he was a knight in shining armour. He made everything clear: the reason for their marriage, the fact that he only desired her . . .

Wrestling with her problems, Lise was unaware of the approach of a tall dark woman round the edge of the pool.

'Hi, I hope you don't mind me barging in like this. I did ring the bell, but there was no answer.'

Lise looked up, shading her eyes from the sun, to find with surprise that the visitor was Diana de la Mesengère.

'Mrs Porter is out doing the weekly shopping,' she heard herself saying, her mind reeling first with shock and then with anger.

'Jordon not about?' Diana asked casually, her eyes drifting curiously over Lise's smooth body, barely concealed by the tiny bikini covering it.

'He's in the city,' Lise replied stiffly, sitting up.

As always, Diana de la Mesengère looked cool and chic and very beautiful. Today her black hair was loose, falling thick and shining to her shoulders. She was wearing fashionable white trousers and a baggy white jacket. Her make-up was perfect, her jewellery understated, and expensive. She looked like something out of *Vogue* and Lise felt grubby and childish in comparison.

'Never mind,' Diana replied, smiling. 'It was you I really came to see.'

Lise shrugged into the short towelling robe that was draped over the back of her sun lounger. She was astounded by the woman's coolness. What on earth was she doing here? Had she come in search of Jordon? Or had she come to deliver a warning?

Briefly Lise wondered whether or not Jordon was still seeing her, or more to the point, still sleeping with her.

She drew herself up to her full height, jealous pain making her angry. 'Madame de la Mesengère——' she began uncomfortably.

'Oh, call me Diana, please,' the other woman laughed. 'I hate formality.'

'What did you want to see me about?' Lise asked, ignoring that, wanting her to get straight to the point, wanting her to leave.

Diana's eyebrows lifted slightly, not mistaking the note in Lise's voice. 'Well, I thought we might get to know each other a little better,' she said gently. 'After all, Jordon is my only brother, and the wedding was such a private affair. However, if you're busy . . .'

Lise was staring at her, wide-eyed, her heart thumping in her chest. '*Brother*?' she echoed weakly, hardly able to take it in.

Diana regarded her, head on one side, eyes amused. 'Yes, brother. What on earth did you think?'

Feeling incredibly foolish, Lise shook her head, her face scarlet with embarrasment. 'Oh—oh, nothing.' She pulled herself together quickly. 'I'm sorry, I'm being very rude. Won't you come inside and have some coffee?'

She gestured towards the house and Diana nodded, still looking at her with questioning eyes. 'Sure, I'd love to.'

Lise led the way, an unwilling smile curving her lips, a crazy happiness bubbling up inside her. She was so stupid! It had never occurred to her for a moment that Diana and Jordon were related. She had immeadiately jumped to the conclusion that they were lovers. She was always ready to think the worst of Jordon and in consequence, had landed herself in another embarrassing situation. What would Diana think of her?

Inside the cool white sitting-room, she asked Diana to sit down. 'I'll make the coffee.'

'Want a hand?' Diana reached inside her handbag and extracted a slim gold cigarette case.

'No, it will only take a minute.'

While she was waiting for the percolator, Lise rushed upstairs, hastily brushed her hair, and dressed in jeans and a matching shirt. She couldn't stop smiling.

By the time she carried the tray into the living-room, she was fully composed. She poured coffee and offered Diana a slice of Mrs Porter's delicious raspberry torte.

'You don't mind me smoking?' Diana asked apologetically.

'No, of course not. I like the smell of French cigarettes,' Lise replied, smiling.

Diana smiled too. 'Do you mind me asking how old you are, Lise?'

'No, I'm twenty-one,' replied Lise evenly. Diana was so sophisticated, she thought wryly. No doubt she saw Lise as little more than a child.

'No wonder Jordon is so protective of you,' Diana said gently.

'Do you think I'm too young for him?' It was important that Diana approved of her.

'Do you love him?'

'Yes.' The answer came without hesitation. Her love shone in her eyes with painful intensity, and Diana's face softened.

'Then no, I don't think you're too young. Renard is fifteen years older than I am. It certainly hasn't made any difference to us.' Her mouth was tender as she spoke of her husband. Lise could see that they obviously shared a happy marriage.

'Jordon said you live in Paris,' she said, liking Diana more and more. She was bright and open and obviously loved talking. She reminded Lise a little of Jerri. 'Is your husband over here with you?'

'Yes, he's in L.A., tied up in boring old conferences for the next few weeks, so I came on to San Francisco to visit friends, and, of course, to see Jordon. You'll have to forgive my nosiness——'

'I don't mind, really,' Lise cut in quickly. 'I'd like us to be friends.'

'So would I, and I'm sure we will be. Jordon has waited a long time to find the right woman, and I knew she'd be someone special.'

Lise flushed, not knowing what to say. Diana obviously didn't know the real reason behind their marriage.

'In fact,' Diana continued, smiling, 'I think I knew that first time we met, remember? At that nightclub? Jordon had insisted on seeing the play you were in, and when I saw you together—oh, I don't know— there was just something about him—about the way he was looking at you.'

Confused by these revelations, which she stored away to examine when she was alone, Lise said, 'You must be very close.'

Diana shrugged. 'In some ways. I idolised him when I was a girl. But he's a very private man, very strong, and strong people are always the most difficult to get close to.'

Lise nodded and something must have shown in her face, because Diana said, 'You are happy, aren't you?'

'Yes,' Lise smiled, her brightest smile, because she didn't want to worry Jordon's sister and because she didn't know her well enough yet to confide in.

'I'm so glad,' Diana said sincerely, believing her. 'For both of you. Jordon has needed somebody like you for a long time.' And when she saw Lise's surprise, she added, 'Oh, I know women fling themselves at him. They always have done and they probably always will. But as his only sister and only living relative, I'm happy that he's finally settled down.'

Lise offered more coffee. It was unsettling to hear Diana talking as though the marriage had been made in heaven. There was nothing she could do but try to bluff her way through.

'Jordon tells me that your parents are dead,' she said unthinkingly, then realised how tactless she was being, her hand flying to her mouth, her eyes embarrassed.

'It's okay,' Diana laughed, trying to put her at ease. 'They died when we were both young. Jordon practically brought me up. I don't suppose he told you that?'

'No, he didn't,' Lise admitted, her curiosity becoming aroused. Apart from the very barest details, she knew very little about his life, and her eyes begged to be told more.

'I was fifteen when my mother died,' Diana obliged dispassionately. 'Jordon was seventeen. Our father was a drunkard and a gambler. We were penniless when my mother died, living in a New York slum. She worked herself to death trying to pay off his debts.' Her mouth twisted with amusement. 'Tell me if I'm boring you; it's no fairy tale.'

'No, go on,' prompted Lise quickly. 'I know hardly anything about Jordon's life.'

'Well, Jordon took on the role provider when she died. He worked in a steel mill to put us through college, and to earn us enough money to live on. It was hard dirty work, and he'd come home almost too exhausted to study for his exams. They were very hard times for both of us, but especially for Jordon. Those years shaped him, hardened him, gave him an incredible inner strength. I saw him change; he became tough and self-sufficient. His life hasn't been easy. He fought his way to the top and now he's one of the most powerful men in America. Not bad for a boy from the slums of the Bronx, huh?' She laughed, lifting her shoulders self-consciously. 'As you can probably tell, I'm very proud of him.'

Lise, who had been listening to every word, fascinated, said quietly, 'You obviously care for him a great deal.'

'I do,' admitted Diana without reserve.

Lise tried to imagine Jordon as a child, then as a young man, having to work all the hours God sent to keep and educate his younger sister and himself. It revealed his strength of character, though it made her heart ache.

'Did you know his wife?' she asked, unable to bite the question back.

'Natalie? He's told you about her?'

Only that he was married, that she died in childbirth.'

Natalie, Lise was thinking. The name conjured up a small, vulnerable girl with long black hair. Beautiful, Lise suspected, gentle and sweet-natured. Everything she wasn't herself.

'It must be love,' Diana said, surprise in her eyes. 'It's not like my brother to talk about his past. He married her when he was twenty, with all the passion of youth. She was a friend of mine, actually.'

'I wonder if he has any photographs of her,' Lise wondered out loud.

Diana shook her head, very sure. 'I doubt it. He leaves the past alone. He's not a sentimental man, though I know it's all still there in his head. He felt as guilty as hell for years after she died. He thought that if he'd had enough money for specialist medical treatment, she and the child would have survived. It wasn't true, of course; the doctors told him that there was nothing *anybody* could have done. It took him a long time to get over it, though if it's any consolation, I think they would have parted if Natalie had lived. They both changed so much. Married too young, I guess.' She lit a cigarette. 'Jordon would kill me if he knew I'd been talking to you like this.'

'I'm glad you told me,' replied Lise, knowing that in Diana she had found a true friend.

'Any time. I'd tell the world what Jordon did for me, because I know damn well he won't blow his own trumpet!' She glanced at the slim gold watch on her wrist. 'God, is that the time? I've been chatting on for ages. You'll have to excuse me: I have a lunch appointment that I can't break.' She threw her cigarette case and lighter back into her handbag. 'I heard that your grandfather is ill again.'

Lise nodded. 'It looks as though he's going to pull through though, thank goodness. I visited him yesterday, and all the signs are good. He's looking much better.'

'That's wonderful news.' Diana stood up. 'I'm glad we finally met for a chat,' she said, in her friendly way. 'Even though I did most of the chatting. It drives Renard *mad* the way I let my mouth run away with me! You and Jordon must come over to dinner as soon as Renard gets back from L.A.'

'Thanks. I'm sure we'd love to.'

'I'll call you,' Diana promised, as she slid behind the wheel of a sleek white Porsche.

Lise watched her go, waving until the car was out of sight. So that is Jordon's sister, she thought, smiling to herself. After this afternoon it was difficult to believe that she had ever imagined them to be lovers. She was probably going out of her mind.

Jordon returned from the city as darkness was falling. Lise was sitting on the veranda staring out into the night, a glass of chilled fruit juice in front of her, She did not hear him approaching, and almost jumped out of her skin as she turned her head and found him watching her.

'You scared me!' she said breathlessly, trying to disguise the fact that his brooding gaze thoroughly unnerved her.

He smiled sardonically. 'Do you want a drink?'

'I have one, thank you.' She lifted the glass of fruit juice, then turned to watch him as he poured himself a measure of Bourbon.

He looked tired and tense, and she ached to put her arms round him, kiss him, like any ordinary wife greeting her husband.

He moved back towards her, easing himself into a chair opposite hers, shrugging out of his jacket and loosening his tie. Their eyes met, and hers dropped immediately, hot colour pouring into her cheeks at her own thoughts.

'Did you have a good day?' Her voice sounded bright and empty in her ears.

The grey eyes narrowed on her face. 'Yes. And you?'

'Your sister visited me.'

Jordon smiled. 'I thought it wouldn't take her long.'

'I liked her,' said Lise quietly.

'Good.' He drained his glass, and she felt the tension in the air.

'Jordon——' She closed her mouth, not sure what she had been about to say.

'What is it?' He leaned across the table, taking her chin between his fingers, forcing her to meet the searching depths of his eyes.

'We hardly know each other,' she whispered anxiously.

'Is that my fault?' he asked, watching her.

'I don't know.' She felt as though she was drowning.

'What the hell do you want, Lise?' His voice was remote, very cool.

Her eyes flickered. 'I don't know,' she said, lying again. 'Kindness, perhaps.'

'You don't think I'm kind?' He smiled mockingly, and when she didn't answer, he said, 'I'd say we know each other pretty well.' His meaning was obvious, and she flushed scarlet.

'Physical response isn't everything.'

'It's all you offer,' he said coldly. 'Since our marriage you've been hiding behind a wall of ice.'

'Do you want more?' she demanded, her temper slipping away from her control.

'I want a wife,' he stated.

'And I'm not a wife?'

'What do you think?' he asked cruelly. 'You resent the fact that I can arouse you. You force me to force you.'

'And you're ruthless!' she cried bitterly, jumping to her feet. 'And hard and cold.'

She whirled away, but Jordon moved very fast, his hand grasping her shoulder, his fingers biting into her flesh.

'You always take,' she flung at him. 'You never give.'

'Then I shall take now,' he said, his voice heavy, as he pulled her up against his body. She felt his tense rigidity as his mouth burned hers, and she fought him, anger exploding inside her.

In response, he held her tighter, his arms intolerably strong, his mouth becoming gentle. He kissed her face slowly, tasting her skin with deliberate sensuality. Lise trembled, the familiar arrows of desire piercing her, leaving her vulnerable.

'You're wrong,' she whispered shakily. 'I've wanted you as much as you've wanted me. It's not a case of force.'

She looked up into his face and found that his eyes were closed, as though he was intensely weary.

'It doesn't matter,' he said harshly. 'When you're in my arms I can think of nothing but you. And right now, I want that oblivion only you can give me.'

Something was nagging away inside her, and she asked shakily, 'Have you made love to anybody else since we married?'

He lifted his head, his grey eyes holding hers. 'No,' he said flatly, and she knew he was telling the truth. The hunger he showed her in bed every night convinced her too. He wasn't seeing anybody else, and the knowledge made her smile with relief.

'Pleased?' His mockery flicked her like a whip.

'It was just idle curiosity,' she retorted coldly. 'So don't flatter yourself.'

That made him laugh, though she could feel his anger. He swung her into his powerful arms, and carried her upstairs to his bed.

Lise lay passive, knowing that to struggle would be futile, and that it only amused him, anyway. He laid her down on the bed, arching over her, his hands on both sides of her head.

She lay staring up into his dark face. It seemed harsh and hardboned in the scented darkness, totally without compassion. His eyes searched her face, and she felt her heart somersaulting wildly.

Slowly Jordon lowered his head, his mouth brushing hers with deliberate slowness, returning again and again, teasing her with brief tender kisses, until she lifted her hands almost mad with hunger, threading them in his black hair to pull down his head.

The kiss changed at once. His mouth plundered hers deeply, achingly, showing her a passion that seemed to be more than just physical need.

'Do you want me?' he murmured against her mouth.

'Yes.' She surrendered weakly, unable to lie.

Jordon smiled, a bitter twisting of his lips. 'Tell me about Paul Lianos.'

Lise froze, her drowsy eyes mirroring her shock. She tried to move her head, but his hands came up to frame her face, holding her still.

'Tell me,' he said again.

'Don't,' she muttered restlessly. 'Kiss me, Jordon, please.'

She lifted her head from the pillows, finding the

hard line of his mouth with her own. She moved her lips against his with pleading gentleness. He didn't respond, refusing to accept what she offered.

Lise closed her eyes against her tears, admitting to herself that she needed his touch, his passion, as much as she needed air to breathe. He had taught her well over the past week, and she had responded wildly, uncaring that his desire was only physical. She needed him to become whole herself, and the knowledge hurt like an open wound.

'Why did you marry me?' she whispered, hiding her tears in the darkness.

'You know why.'

'Yes. Holbrook International.' Her voice was deathly. It was the answer she deserved.

Jordon shifted so that he was lying beside her. 'What did he do to you?' he demanded, staring up at the ceiling.

'I don't want to talk about Paul Lianos——'

'I do. I want to know just how involved you are with him.' The words were spoken with calm tenacity.

Lise sighed, squeezing her eyes tight shut. She couldn't tell him, she just couldn't.

Jordon reached out and switched on the light. He saw the tears trickling down her pale face, the furrows of pain on her forehead.

'Tell me, Lise,' he ordered softly.

'Jordon, please——'

'Open your eyes! Look at me, goddammit!' His anger vibrated around the room.

She turned away, refusing to obey the command, terrified that he would read the answers he wanted if she showed him her eyes.

A few seconds of silence ticked by, then she heard

him swearing violently under his breath. She felt the mattress give and knew that he was getting up. She felt very cold.

As he reached the door, she opened her eyes. 'Where are you going?' she asked, feeling terribly insecure.

'To do some work,' he said bleakly. Then the door was slammed and he was gone.

CHAPTER TEN

THREE days later, Lise visited her grandfather in hospital.

Nancy picked her up from Jordon's house and they went together. The promised play from Victor Jamal had arrived that morning, but Lise barely had the heart to look at it. She wanted the part, in fact she longed to get back to work again, but a curious depressed lethargy held her in its grip.

Jordon hadn't touched her since walking out the night they argued, and she lay alone in the bed every night aching with frustration, unable to sleep. He seemed to be working longer and longer hours in the city, and, weak with longing for him, she couldn't help imagining, in the dark hours before dawn broke, that he must be seeing another woman.

When they spent time together, he treated her with chilling politeness, as though she was a stranger in his house. She knew why: he suspected her to be involved with Paul Lianos and she deliberately let him think that in a desperate effort to save the last remnants of her pride. She knew how damning it looked, but she couldn't bring herself to tell him the truth.

This morning, Jordon had already gone when she came downstairs, dull and heavy-eyed after another restless night. The only evidence that he had been in the dining-room at all was a hastily folded newspaper and an empty coffee cup. Lise had broken down in tears, hastily wiping her face as Mrs Porter appeared with fruit juice and fresh coffee.

She felt lost and very lonely, glad to see Nancy when she arrived in Mason's car.

'You look tired,' observed Nancy, not unkindly, as the car purred towards the city.

'I couldn't sleep last night,' Lise answered truthfully. It seemed that her careful make-up hadn't fooled the older woman for a second. Nancy didn't say anything else, and for the rest of the journey they chatted about Lise's prospects of joining the Sausalito Theatre company.

Mason was looking much better when they arrived. He eyed Lise keenly. 'Happy with Jordon Hayes?' he demanded brusquely.

Lise tried to smile. 'Yes.' Another lie. How many would she have to tell? she wondered.

'Guilty conscience?' queried Nancy wryly.

'Don't be ridiculous,' he replied, but when Nancy left the room in search of Louis Salvador, he said to Lise, 'You look like death, girl. Not treating you badly, is he?'

'He's treating me very well,' she replied with dignity. As she looked at him, she still wondered how he could have done it. She knew that it was in his nature, and that he probably thought he had done the right thing, but it still hurt, and it would be a long time before she could forgive him. It was incredible that an intelligent man like Mason could be so blind, so inept at judging people's feelings.

'Good. Good. It's for the best. At the very least, your future is secure.'

Lise felt like laughing. She had never felt more insecure in her life.

'You're looking great,' she said, changing the

subject. Whatever he had done, she still cared for him.

'I'll be out of here as soon as I can.'

'And what will you do?'

He grinned, almost like a boy. 'Ask Nancy! She's got everything worked out.'

'It's about time somebody took you in hand,' she said, laughing. 'You've had your own way for far too long.'

'Maybe.' From the look on his face, she had the feeling that it wasn't going to be easy for Nancy.

As they were leaving, he halted them at the door, his eyes holding Lise's. 'You know, I really thought I was going to die this time.'

It was the nearest he had ever come to an apology or an explanation, and Lise nodded. 'I know.' She believed him too, perhaps because she wanted to so much.

Over lunch with Nancy at a French restaurant in Ghirardelli Square, she said, 'What's Mason going to do when he gets out of hospital? He said you have everything worked out.'

Nancy laughed. 'And he can't stand it!'

'I'll bet. What's your plan?'

'Retirement in Hawaii,' revealed Nancy.

'Retirement? Mason?' Lise's eyes widened incredulously.

'Why not? Now that he's lost the company, there's nothing to keep him in San Francisco. If I let him stay here, he'll be back in business within six months.'

Lise nodded, and Nancy continued, 'I've stood by for too long and watched him trying to work himself into an early grave. But no more. I've leased a house on Molokai. We'll be leaving as soon as Louis gives me the word that Mason is fit to travel.'

Lise lifted her wine glass in salute. 'You really have got it all worked out. It's wonderful news, Nancy, really wonderful!'

'I hope so. He's always professed a passion for fishing; now he'll have the chance to try his hand.' Nancy's eyes were glowing with amusement. 'I'm only hoping that the old devil will mellow out there in all that tropical sunshine. Twenty years is a long time to wait for a proposal.'

Lise's fork had halted halfway between her plate and her mouth. 'I *knew* you were in love with him,' she declared with delight. 'Oh, Nancy, good luck! I can't think of anyone who deserves happiness more than you.'

'Thank you, darling.' The older woman's eyes were wet with tears. 'I hope you wish your grandfather the same luck. He's not a bad man, Lise, really he isn't. He just finds it hard to express his feelings.'

Lise nodded. How many times had she heard Nancy defending him? she wondered sadly. 'I know. But my pride has taken a terrible beating, and that's not easy to forgive.'

'What do you mean?' Nancy seemed genuinely puzzled.

'Oh, you don't have to pretend. Meredith very kindly told me about the deal Grandpa cooked up with Jordon. I was sold off like a parcel of shares.'

Nancy shook her head. 'Meredith is nothing more than a trouble-making bitch!' she declared angrily. 'I'm going to have a few well-chosen words for that girl when I see her!'

'It's not worth it,' said Lise quietly. 'She told me the truth and that's all that really matters.'

'Has it caused trouble between you and Jordon?'

asked Nancy perceptively.

Lise sighed. 'It certainly hasn't made things any easier. Every time I look at him, I know that he was practically forced to marry me——'

'*What?*'

'I said every time I——'

'Just what did Meredith tell you?' demanded Nancy incredulously.

Frowning, Lise said, 'That Jordon had wanted Holbrook International for years and that when Mason realised that he was going to have to sell, securing my future was part of the deal. Meredith called it an attack of conscience.'

'And if that was true, why do you think Jordon agreed to it?' Nancy asked crisply.

Lise shrugged. 'I suppose Mason could have made the takeover more difficult. He could have sold to someone else . . .'

She could feel the tears welling up in her eyes. It hurt like hell to talk about it at all, let alone try to work out Jordon's motives.

Nancy was smiling. 'Now you listen to me, my girl, and listen carefully.'

'Nancy, I don't really want to talk——'

'Listen! Meredith was lying through her teeth! It was common knowledge that she had her sights set on Jordon, all the more desperately when she realised that he was taking over Holbrook International. Jordon never seemed particularly interested in her, although, of course, he was always polite.'

'But I thought . . . She said . . .'

'I can imagine what she said! Don't you recognise jealous spite when you see it? You arrived here and it became obvious to anyone with eyes in their head that it was you Jordon wanted.'

Lise frowned, turning over what Nancy was telling her. She found it impossible to believe Jordon did want her—had wanted her, she amended painfully—but anyway, it had been a purely physical desire. It had never for a moment been love.

'I don't know——' she began doubtfully.

'Well, I do,' replied Nancy firmly. 'Why do you think Mason feels so guilty? I was in on the negotiations for the takeover, remember. I knew exactly how much trouble the company was in, and believe me, Jordon was in a position to call all the shots. Mason had to acquiesce to all his demands.'

'You mean . . .?'

'I mean that Meredith turned it all round. *He* wanted *you*,' insisted Nancy. 'He wanted to marry you, or no deal.'

'I don't believe it!' Lise began to smile, her face suddenly radiant.

'Oh, it's true. I played hell with Mason about it. It seemed so—Victorian! I played hell—until I realised that you were in love with Jordon. Mason was all for it, but not for the reasons you think. He's always loved you, and he *did* want to make sure that your future was safe. Remember, he's lost almost everything.'

Lise felt like laughing out loud. Now that she knew the truth, she could even forgive Meredith for being so spiteful. She felt strong and suddenly hopeful. She would get through to Jordon. Somehow, she would make him realise that she loved him.

As they finished lunch, she said, 'I'll get a taxi back. There's something I have to do in the city.'

'Are you sure?'

'Yes. And thank you, Nancy, thank you for everything.'

Nancy's eyes were wise and happy. 'Be happy, darling. Make it work.'

'I will,' promised Lise fervently. 'I will.'

The towering office block that housed Jordon's bank stood on Montgomery Street, in the heart of the financial district of the city. Lise's taxi drew up in front of it, and as she leaned forward to pay the driver she froze at what she saw through the window.

Through the revolving glass doors of the building walked Meredith and Jordon, moving towards a long black limousine that stood at the kerb. Meredith was smiling, her hand on Jordon's arm. Lise's stunned eyes moved to the face of her husband. He showed no expression as he stood back to let Meredith climb into the back of the car. He closed the door, and walked back into the office building as the car purred slowly away, up towards Nob Hill. It all happened in a matter of seconds, but in Lise's mind, it repeated itself over and over again.

The taxi driver was staring at her as though she had gone mad, and she apologised and told him to take her home. He lifted his shoulders at her incomprehensible behaviour, as he slammed the car into gear. 'You okay, lady?' he demanded, watching her through the rear view mirror.

'Fine,' replied Lise through her teeth, angrier than she had ever been in her life. She had nearly made a terrible fool of herself. Nancy must have been wrong, Meredith right, she thought wildly.

And Jordon—her heart twisted. Jordon had lied. He had been seeing Meredith all the time.

By the time she got home, a cold numbness had

settled over her, almost blotting out her anger. She wandered aimlessly through the rooms of the house, wondering what she should do. Nothing occurred to her; it was as though her mind had stopped functioning the moment she had seen Jordon leaving his office with Meredith.

She was in the bedroom when she heard the doorbell chiming. She ignored it, sitting curled up on the end of the bed, her green eyes totally blank. Moments later, she heard Mrs Porter's quiet knock on the door.

'There's a gentleman downstairs to see you, Mrs Hayes,' the housekeeper said with a warm smile. 'A Mr Paul Lianos.'

Lise lifted her head. 'Did he say what he wanted?' she asked dully, unable to feel surprised, only irritated at the intrusion.

'Well, no.' Mrs Porter seemed taken aback by the question. 'But he seemed anxious to see you.'

'Tell him——' She tried to think of something, but couldn't. 'Oh, it doesn't matter, I'll come down.'

The housekeeper nodded and walked towards the door, then turned, her face troubled. 'I hope you don't mind me asking . . . but . . . are you feeling all right, Mrs Hayes?'

'Yes, thank you Mrs Porter—a little tired, that's all.' Lise forced a smile and it seemed to satisfy the housekeeper.

Looking down at her cream skirt and silk blouse, she decided that Paul Lianos wasn't worth the trouble of changing for, and made her way downstairs.

He was standing in the living-room, staring out of the windows, his hands stuffed into the trouser pockets of his light suit. Lise looked at him with cold dislike as she entered the room.

'What do you want?' she demanded without preamble. She felt protected from any fears of him by the icy mantle that cloaked her. He turned, his insolent glance raking her from head to toe.

'Now, what do you think?' he asked, smiling. 'You didn't return my call.'

'Was I expected to?' All the contempt she felt for him was in her voice. How she could ever have imagined herself in love with him, even for a second, was beyond her comprehension. She despised him because he had ruined her young life and he didn't care. He probably didn't even know.

'You always did play hard to get,' he said confidently. 'How about dinner tonight?'

'No,' she replied icily. 'I'm a married woman, or didn't you know that?' She walked towards the door. 'I'd like you to leave.'

He didn't move. He stared at her and the hot excitement in his blue eyes made her feel sick.

'Don't turn me down, Lise,' he said, using his charm, charm she had once responded to so innocently. 'I want to get to know you again. I tried to find you, you know, but you'd disappeared off the face of the earth.'

'Get out!' she repeated, her hands clenching at her sides.

'You don't want your husband to find me here?' he suggested softly. 'Don't worry, I can be very discreet.' He walked towards her. As three years ago, he couldn't accept her rejection of him.

She could see the anger and the hurt pride in his face. His hands gripped her shoulders, and she thought, I'll die if he touches me. I'll never be able to wash myself clean.

'Let me go,' she said, but her voice was shaking.

Paul Lianos laughed, looking down into her deathly pale face. 'I don't think you mean that, sweetheart.'

'I want you to get out, now!' she repeated through chattering teeth.

You heard the lady. I suggest you do as she asks,' Jordon's cold voice broke between them.

Lise turned her head and met his silvery eyes. She hadn't heard him come in, but she suddenly felt safe. Paul Lianos couldn't hurt her now.

Paul Lianos released her, turning to Jordon, a carefully arrogant smile on his face. But Lise saw something else in his eyes. He was frightened of Jordon, she realised with satisfaction, and she wasn't surprised. Jordon looked ready to commit murder.

'Get out of here.' The words were spoken with a soft savagery, and Paul Lianos flinched, though his face was still set in a mask of insolent amusement. He held up his hands.

'Okay, I'm going.' He gave himself away, moving too fast towards the door, not even glancing at Lise.

As the front door slammed and a car engine roared into life, Lise let out her breath on a sigh of pure relief. She looked at Jordon and found him watching her, a ferocious anger burning in his eyes.

'You're ... you're back early,' she stammered, nerves fluttering in her stomach.

'I'm sorry if that inconveniences you,' he drawled icily.

'I didn't mean ... thank you, for what you did.' Her face was burning.

'What did I do?' He walked towards her, and she sensed that every movement was tightly controlled.

Her glance flickered nervously. 'You know very well. I didn't invite him here, if that's what you're thinking,' she retorted, annoyed by her own timidity.

'I can believe that,' he said, his mouth twisting. 'You're shaking like a leaf.'

Lise wrapped her arms protectively around her body.

'I despise him,' she whispered brokenly.

'Did he hurt you?' Jordon's icy glance flicked over her, inspecting every inch of her face and body.

'I don't think he could,' she said scornfully.

'He did once, though, didn't he?'

Lise turned away, walking over to the windows. 'Yes,' she admitted. 'Once.'

'How?' The question was fired at her like a bullet from a gun, but she sensed that he had controlled his anger, forced himself to relax.

'Why do you ask? I don't ask you about your past affairs.' Something inside her still held back from telling him the whole story.

'You don't find my past affairs in the house when you come home,' he replied evenly.

No, Lise thought bitterly. Your affairs are conducted with great discretion. She said nothing.

'Tell me, Lise,' said Jordon, an almost pleading note in his voice. 'I think I can guess most of it now, but I'd like to hear it from you.'

She looked round, her soft hair swinging, catching the sunlight. 'All right!' He had worn her down. She was tired of holding the secret. She looked up into his cool grey eyes. 'I'd like a drink though, first.'

He nodded, pouring out two measures of Scotch, handing one to her. She sipped it gratefully, the fiery spirit burning her throat. She was aware that his eyes didn't leave her face for a second and for some strange reason, that gave her strength.

'I was eighteen,' she began. 'Just out of college, and so naïve, you wouldn't have believed it. Mason was keen to get me married off—advantageously, of course—and Paul Lianos was his choice.'

Jordon stiffened. Lise felt the movement without raising her eyes from the carpet.

'Mason threw us together at a party,' she continued tonelessly. 'I drank too much champagne. Paul cornered me in Mason's study. He ... He ...' She found that she couldn't frame the words.

'He raped you?' Jordon asked, his voice raw.

'No. I think he would have done, but I managed to fight him off.' She swallowed back the Scotch, and tried to laugh, failing miserably. 'And that's it—not exactly the crime of the century!'

She looked at him then, waiting for his pity or his contempt, very exposed. It didn't come. She could almost see his mind working everything out, and she could see his anger.

'The bastard!' he said through his teeth. 'I'll kill him!'

He moved towards the door, his body taut, violence emanating in waves from him.

Lise grabbed his arm. 'No!' she cried. 'Jordon, don't! He's not worth it ... I'm free of him now, don't you see? He won't come back here, you frightened him to death.' She was afraid that he would end up in jail.

'Why should you want to protect him?'

'Not him, *you*!' she replied fiercely. 'He's not worth it.'

'I'm going to make him pay for what he did to you,' he told her, but she had stopped him for the moment.

His eyes darkened as he searched her pale face. 'Oh, Lise, why didn't you tell me this before? You shouldn't have kept it bottled up inside you.'

'I was afraid,' she said shakily, realising that he was right. Now that she had told him, a great weight had been lifted from her shoulders. The wound was finally beginning to heal, exposed at last to the air and the light.

'Of what?' he asked gently, stroking back her hair from her face.

'I was afraid——' She shrugged, responding to the touch of his hand with trembling awareness.

'That it would change the way I feel about you?' Jordon framed her face with his hands. 'Not a chance, love. It doesn't make a blind bit of difference, except to make me wish I could have prevented it.' The tenderness in his voice soothed her aching heart, her self-inflicted shame and embarrassment.

Then, like a nightmare she remembered what she had seen today. Jordon and Meredith. Together. Scalded with pain at his deceit, she pulled away from him, putting distance between them. Jordon let her go, his narrowed eyes following her.

'What is it?' His shoulders were set in a tense line, weariness etched his face. It would never be right between them, Lise thought defeatedly. There were too many lies. If she stayed, he would destroy her, she would destroy herself.

'I want to leave here,' she said, not knowing how she kept her voice so even. 'I want a divorce.'

Nothing showed in his eyes. 'No,' he stated harshly. 'I have no intention of letting you go. Not now, not ever.'

'Why not?' she cried in anguish. 'You've got the

company now, you don't need me.'

'Don't I?' He took a deep breath, controlling his temper with difficulty. 'Dammit, Lise, how can you be so blind?' He walked from the room, slamming the door so hard that the whole house seemed to shake.

Lise stared after him and for a second what he had said didn't sink in. When it did, she sank down on to the sofa, her legs giving way under her. Had he really said that he needed her? She pressed a trembling hand to her mouth. She knew what she wanted to do, but—— Her thoughts halted, realisation hitting her. She was free now, she could follow her impulses. Take a chance, a voice inside her head was urging, take a chance.

Jordon had healed her, made her strong, able to love with an intensity that terrified her. She couldn't let that go.

She jumped to her feet, running up the stairs in search of her husband.

The bedroom was empty, but from the bathroom she could hear the hissing of the shower. Without thinking, she pushed open the bathroom door.

The glass shower cubicle stood in one corner of the bathroom, separate from the bath. Through the frosted panes she could see Jordon. He had his back to her, his arms above his head, as he leant against the tiles, water cascading over him.

The nameless defeat she could see in the broad sweep of his back and the tense set of his shoulders, made her heart lurch violently. At the mercy of her emotions, she slid out of her clothes, and tugging open the glass door, walked naked into the shower.

Jordon turned quickly, drawing a long uneven breath as he saw her. Lise flushed to the roots of her hair, as his grey glance moved with slow hunger over her body. She looked at him. His black hair was plastered to his head. The light gleamed on the tanned strength of his shoulders, and the hair that matted his chest was beaded with droplets of water.

'I love you,' she whispered, finally abandoning her stupid pride.

'Tell me again,' he said huskily.

Lise put her hand out and touched his chest. He tensed, the muscles contracting under his wet skin, and she moved closer, feeling the hot water pouring over her body like a dam bursting.

Her hand slid upwards to his shoulder, to his neck. 'I love you,' she said again, and kissed him.

At the touch of her mouth, he groaned, his own arms coming around her tightly.

'I've waited a lifetime to hear you say that,' he muttered against her lips. 'God, I love you, Lise! I fell in love with you the moment I saw you.'

The kiss deepened, hunger flaring between them, out of control. Lise offered him everything she had held back before, her mouth openly erotic beneath his.

Jordon shuddered as she caressed him, his heart racing heavily beneath her hands. He lifted her against his body, his powerful muscles supporting her easily and she gasped with pleasure, crying out his name as he possessed her.

With the water streaming over them, they made love, their mouths clinging hungrily. Her passion matched his as he brought them both to an ecstatic culmination of desire, so intense that Lise almost fainted in his arms.

Afterwards they soaped each other with lazy sensuality. Jordon dried her skin with a huge white towel, his hands gentle, then led her to bed.

She lay with her head against his chest, his arms around her. The ferocity of their lovemaking had exhausted her, sated her. At last, the frustrations of three long nights alone, were released.

'I saw you with Meredith today, outside your office,' Lise said drowsily.

'What were you doing outside my office?' Jordon asked, his mouth against her hair.

'I was coming to see you. What was she doing there?'

'She came to see me for a job. I sent her packing. She may be your cousin, my love, but I loathe her.'

Lise smiled. 'The day we married, she hinted to me that you and she were lovers.'

Jordon tilted up her face so that he could see her eyes. 'I've never touched her—never wanted to. You do believe me?'

'Yes. She was just trying to make trouble—I know that now.'

Jordon kissed her face, closing her eyes, his mouth finally touching hers.

'Was it a coincidence that you were at the last night of the play?' she asked, shivering as his lips moved to her throat.

'No,' he admitted unashamedly. 'I was intrigued by the girl who had given up the Holbrook fortune. The moment I laid eyes on you, I knew that you were the one I'd been waiting for. It seemed like fate.'

'You scared me,' confessed Lise, smiling. 'You were so sure, so strong. I'd never met anybody like you.'

Jordon laughed. 'You didn't show it! You seemed totally indifferent to me, except when we kissed. Your response was the only thing that gave me hope.' He smiled wryly. 'I thought I had all the time in the world. I thought I'd be able to take it slowly, but I couldn't control my impatience or my damned jealousy.'

'Jealousy?' asked Lise incredulously, touching the tip of her tongue to his bare shoulder, revelling in his involuntary response.

'Yes, jealousy. I was jealous of Ashley, of Shaun Barnett, of Lianos—of every man that looked at you. You have a curiously untouched air that any man would find fascinating. I was getting nowhere with you, and I was afraid I was going to lose you'

Lise laughed. 'I hadn't looked at a man in three years, until you. I fell in love with you so quickly, so deeply . . . there's never been a chance that you would lose me.' She saw his expression, and said, 'You do believe me, don't you?'

'I have to,' he said harshly. 'Otherwise I'd go out of my mind.' 'It would have taken more than Mason trying to extract a deathbed promise out of me to make me marry a man I didn't love,' she whispered, revelling in the hard strength of his chest, running her hands over the short dark hairs that lay against his skin.

Jordon shuddered, his arms tightening around her. 'I love you,' he murmured against her mouth. 'And I want you, Lise, now.'

Their mouths fused, Lise unashamedly showing him her own need, her own desire. Finally he lifted his head, smiling into her drowning eyes.

'I was clumsy with you, Lise, and I'm sorry. I have no excuse to offer except my own desperation. I told Mason I wanted to marry you, I forced his hand. He must have thought I was crazy! When you spotted Lianos in that restaurant, I had to move quickly. I thought you were in love with him. As soon as we married, you started talking about annulment. I had to make sure you had no grounds for it.'

'How ruthless,' she teased softly, wanting to tell him her side of things. 'Oh, Jordon, I was in love with you before I left London, but when I arrived here Meredith warned me off. She said, well, you know what she said. She told me that it was Mason who forced the marriage, not you. That's why I let you think I was involved with Paul.'

Jordon's jaw clenched. 'That bitch! I can't believe she tried so hard to split us up.'

Lise touched his face. 'It doesn't matter. Nancy put me straight.' She paused, then said, 'Perhaps Meredith is in love with you?'

Jordon laughed. 'In love with my money perhaps, not with me. I made it clear to her that I wasn't interested right from the start.'

Lise could find it in her heart to feel sorry for her cousin now. Going to Jordon to ask him for a job meant that she hadn't given up yet, but Lise didn't care any more. Looking into the burning depths of her husband's eyes, she saw a love there that was as hot as the sun, a deep, strong, all-encompassing love that would hold her secure for as long as they both lived.

'You should have told me you loved me,' she said artlessly.

Jordon kissed her hungrily. 'I thought I'd given myself away a thousand times. A man is entitled to a little pride, surely? I thought you knew that I had insisted on our marriage. You seemed to hate me.' There was a note of pain in his deep voice that made her cling to him. 'I was trying to steel myself up to offering you your freedom. I vowed that I wouldn't make love to you again unless you showed me that you wanted it.'

'Oh, Jordon, I thought you'd satisfied your curiosity about me. I thought you didn't want me any more,' she whispered, her heart in her eyes.

He moved lithely, rolling, so that she lay beneath him.

'Never,' he muttered, bending his head to kiss her breasts. 'I'll never have enough of you. I love you, Lise; I'll always love you.'

'And I love you,' she groaned, dissolving in pure sensation as he began to make love to her.

'I'll need some convincing of that,' he smiled, his mouth against her skin.

Later, they would talk again, voicing all the questions that needed answering. But now wasn't the time for talking, it was the time to express a powerful love.

The sun was beginning its slow descent above the trees, the sky slashed with brilliant colours. It filled the quiet room with a deep golden light, and it filled Lise's heart with happiness as she slid her arms around the man she would always love.

Harlequin Presents

Coming Next Month

991 ROSE-COLOURED LOVE Amanda Carpenter
A novelist who has stopped writing because of an unhappy love affair is
confronted in Maine by a strong-willed editor who wants her to write—and
love—again.

992 THE MARRIAGE BED Catherine George
A dream vacation in Portugal turns into a nightmare for a secretary
unexpectedly held captive in a farmhouse by a mysterious, handsome
stranger—who's mistaken her for someone else!

993 SONG IN A STRANGE LAND Diana Hamilton
A Shropshire girl returns home and encounters the man who tricked her years
ago with promises of love. How she'd paid for that brief happiness. So why
does he act as if she mistreated him?

994 RESEARCH INTO MARRIAGE Penny Jordan
A successful English author who doesn't believe in love marries a doctor, a man
embittered by women, yet needing a wife. Somehow their practical marriage
becomes a loving relationship that shatters all their theories and constraints!

995 THE MARRIED LOVERS Flora Kidd
When her wealthy husband telephones about her mother's illness, Sandra, an
English librarian, reluctantly returns to Venice and the man she'd left because
of his deceit. She can't help wondering if this is just another trick.

996 LEAVE YESTERDAY BEHIND Lynsey Stevens
A secretary with a teenage son in Brisbane marries without revealing a secret
from her past—a secret that is connected with her husband. She lives in fear
that he will find out—and of his reaction!

997 TIGER IN HIS LAIR Sally Wentworth
Hurt and humiliated by love, Romily heads for the sanctuary of her brother's
hotel in Scotland. But it's not long before a devastatingly attractive Highland
laird exerts his bewitching—and dangerous—charm on her.

998 UNFINISHED BUSINESS Nicola West
Why would Verity, a woman so desirous of marriage and family, keep turning
down proposals from eminently suitable men? The reasons are buried deep in
her past, and Verity becomes determined to dig them out....

Available in July wherever paperback books are sold, or through Harlequin
Reader Service:

In the U.S.
901 Fuhrmann Blvd.
P.O. Box 1397
Buffalo, N.Y. 14240-1397

In Canada
P.O. Box 603
Fort Erie, Ontario
L2A 5X3

Take 4 books & a surprise gift FREE

SPECIAL LIMITED-TIME OFFER

Mail to   **Harlequin Reader Service®**

In the U.S.   In Canada
901 Fuhrmann Blvd.   P.O. Box 609
P.O. Box 1394   Fort Erie, Ontario
Buffalo, N.Y. 14240-1394   L2A 5X3

YES! Please send me 4 free Harlequin Romance® novels and my free surprise gift. Then send me 8 brand-new novels every month as they come off the presses. Bill me at the low price of $1.99 each*—an 11% saving off the retail price. There are no shipping, handling or other hidden costs. There is no minimum number of books I must purchase. I can always return a shipment and cancel at any time. Even if I never buy another book from Harlequin, the 4 free novels and the surprise gift are mine to keep forever.   118 BPR BP7F

*Plus 89¢ postage and handling per shipment in Canada.

Name _____ (PLEASE PRINT) _____

Address _____ Apt. No. _____

City _____ State/Prov. _____ Zip/Postal Code _____

This offer is limited to one order per household and not valid to present subscribers. Price is subject to change.   DOR-SUB-1D

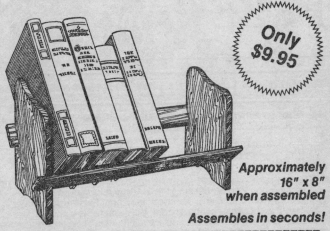

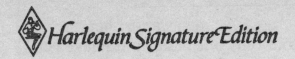

Carole Mortimer

Merlyn's Magic

She came to him from out of the storm and was drawn into his yearning arms—the tempestuous night held a magic all its own.

You've enjoyed Carole Mortimer's Harlequin Presents stories, and her previous bestseller, *Gypsy*.

Now, don't miss her latest, most exciting bestseller, *Merlyn's Magic*!

IN JULY